The Royers of Renfrew

- *A*
Family
Tapestry -

Marie Lanser Beck and Maxine Beck

The past is a foreign country;
they do things differently there.

L.P. Hartley

Little Antietam Press, LLC

Published in the United States

For Nancy Pascoe
who knows a thing
or two about
"taming a wilderness"
Enjoy this journey to 1812.
All good wishes,
Marie Lansew Beck
October 2011

Dedication

Dedicated to the staff and volunteers of Renfrew Institute for Cultural and Environmental Studies and the Renfrew Museum and Park in grateful appreciation for their interpretation of, and care for the historic house and farmstead that were the inspiration for our story

Acknowledgements

No work of fiction can ever see the light of day without the guidance, assistance, encouragement and loving attention freely given by family, friends and colleagues.

The Royers of Renfrew – A Family Tapestry benefited mightily from early readings by gifted editor Dennis Shaw; and historian, author and former Washington County Museum of Fine Arts Curator Jean Woods. Special appreciation goes to Bonnie Iseminger of Renfrew Museum and Park, and Melodie Anderson-Smith of the Renfrew Institute for Cultural and Environmental Studies, the entity that re-created Renfrew's Four-Square Garden in 1994 – the inspiration for this work of fiction.

We are grateful to Katherine Beck Rozes who provided editorial feedback, Linda Zimmerman who helped us navigate German usage, and John Howard McClellan and Kenton Broyles, who provided information about the Bell family pottery. Kristen Adams assisted with interior layout design. We are indebted to Patricia Gaffney and literary agent Alec Shane of Writer's House for their assistance and encouragement and to emergency room physician/author Dr. D. Bruce Foster for his technical advice on publishing.

Waynesboro's Alexander Hamilton Memorial Free Library enabled us to access sources far afield through the magic of inter-library loan, and J&M Printing of Waynesboro provided assistance with scanned images.

Photographer Andrew Gehman provided the cover photography, and Maxine Beck produced the interior illustrations. Special thanks to Tracy Holiday and Sherry Hesse of Renfrew Institute for the loan of authentic period clothes and accessories for our cover girl and niece, Ryleigh Beck.

Any errors in our re-imagining of life on the Royer Farmstead are clearly our own. We hope our depiction of life two centuries ago will give visitors who wander Renfrew's 107 acres today a better appreciation for the trials and triumphs of the Pennsylvania Germans who tamed a wild land to make a home for religious freedom and a livelihood for their families.

This book is a tribute to our Scotch-Irish heritage and our husbands' Pennsylvania German ancestors.

Marie Lanser Beck and Maxine Beck
Waynesboro, Pennsylvania
October 2011

Authors' Notes

A Note on the Use of the Word Indians

In this more language-sensitive era, the words Indians and, especially, savages, are seldom used to describe the vast numbers of native peoples who dominated North America a scant three hundred years ago. But in 1812, on the Pennsylvania frontier, the year this narrative begins, Indians would have been a constant source of fear and danger for the settlers. During the 18th and early 19th centuries, families settling at the edge of the European expansion were engaged in an epic struggle between colonizers, and those resisting colonization.

The Pennsylvania Germans, and to an even greater extent, the Scotch-Irish, attempted to establish a toehold in the fertile valleys along the Appalachian Mountains. These settlers were caught up in the inherent conflict between the two groups during the mid-1700s and beyond. These tensions were further aggravated by the British and French, who enlisted Indian allies in their competing attempts to extract resources from the vast New World.

Brutal attacks on European settlers, and retaliatory raids against the Indians occurred frequently in the Cumberland Valley in Pennsylvania and Maryland during the 1750s. In addition, European political struggles migrated to the disputed territories during the series of conflicts known collectively as The French and Indian War, which resulted not only in the deaths of colonial settlers, but devastated countless Native Americans who suffered, died, or fled West in advance of European expansion.

As apocryphal as the story of the Renfrew sisters massacre in 1764 along the banks of the Antietam Creek may be, the threat Indians posed to those settling what was then America's western frontier was very real.

A Note on Religion

Religion played a major role in every aspect of the lives of Pietist Pennsylvania Germans who fled Europe to escape religious persecution. The Bible was the primary book governing their lives, and devotion to their principles and their community of believers was central to their daily lives. Children were given religious instruction in their homes from an early age, and everything from the layout of the four-square garden to the religious holidays that determined the planting of crops was influenced by the dictates of their conservative Protestant sect.

A Note on Language

At the time of this narrative, the Royers would have spoken German exclusively in their home. But given their farmstead's role in the commerce of Waynesburg, and the region, family members had contact with their English neighbors, and needed to be able to communicate.

In addition, many newspapers and almanacs were published in German to cater to the many German settlers in the mid-Atlantic region. These publications were readily available to Daniel Royer and his family. Both girls and boys in the Royer household were taught to read and write in German.

In this narrative, German phrases and expressions have been included to give readers a sense of the sound and rhythm of the German spoken by the Royers, and among the Pennsylvania Germans who, though most heavily concentrated in Pennsylvania, also settled in parts of Maryland and Virginia. These selected words and phrases are in italics to help the reader differentiate them from the rest of the text.

Contents

A Family Tapestry

-1-

THE ROYER FARMSTEAD

Winters could be 'colder than a witch's elbow' in the valley along the east branch of Little Antietam Creek near the small village of Waynesburg, Pennsylvania, but this late March morning in 1812 offered up a welcome sampler of the newly-arrived spring. Nine-year-old Susan Royer sat by the rushing creek below her home and smiled to herself as she recalled Mrs. McBride's odd description of the colder season three months earlier. The Royers' plain-speaking Scotch-Irish neighbor had wandered past the millpond in mid-January when the water had frozen to ice skating thickness and Susan and her siblings were reaping some enjoyment from the bleak winter.

Today the small stream, lifeblood of the Royer farmstead, burbled under a canopy of newly-budding trees along with the chorus of returning spring robins as Susan lingered along its banks. Sitting on a large limestone slab near the bank, she drew her knees up to her chin and hugged her legs under the layers of her linsey-woolsey skirt and homespun work apron. Her long, light-brown hair was drawn behind her ears into tight braids that dangled on either side of her small white bonnet and came to rest on her hunched shoulders.

The soil in this more temperate area of the Commonwealth had already thawed enough to allow some tilling and planting for the new growing season. The farmstead's large flax crop was already sewn. Susan envisioned her assigned workstation in the Pennsylvania German four-square garden near the two-story log farmhouse she shared with her parents, Daniel and Catherine Royer, and her various siblings – nine of them, from brother, David, 22, to three-month-old Nancy.

Moments alone were rare given the close confines of their 24-by-24-foot cabin and the number of people living in it. While the cabin was sometimes too small for all the souls within, Susan could only be grateful for her many brothers and sisters who shared in the never-ending chores associated with the day-to-day operation of their thriving homestead. Susan's stolen moment of solitude was a welcome benefit to her mother's request to gather enough watercress for the noon meal and to fetch a bucket of fresh water to supplement what came from the small indoor kitchen pump.

In addition to the farming that supplied both food and medicinal herbs, the smelly, family tannery located upstream from where she sat had produced quality leather for some 18 years and the Royer's massive gristmill, completed just four years before, ground local grains to flour and meal from sunrise to sunset during the harvest season. The mill was a big boost to the family income because her father, Daniel, and his miller, Amos  Fahnestock, received a tenth of the grain as payment for the grinding. Many local farmers brought their grains to the Royers for grinding, and "city folk" who didn't have enough land to grow their own crops bought the flour that Daniel didn't need at the town market. It took five bushels of wheat to make one barrel of flour. A lot of grain passed down the wooden chutes through the noisy mill, but her Papa always said that the loud rumble of the heavy round stones was the 'sound of gold.'

Evidence of the family's increasing wealth was visible for all the world to see in the construction of a beautiful two-story home of silvery gray fieldstone quarried from their own acreage. The substantial farmhouse would soon take the place of the familiar log house where each of Daniel and Catherine Royer's 13 children – the ones who had lived and the ones who hadn't lived long – had been born. Susan was fascinated by each stage that brought their new dwelling nearer to completion. One of the upper story rooms had been promised as a bedroom solely for her younger sisters, Rebecca and Cate, and herself. As it was, crossing the main room of the cabin without stepping on a younger sister or bumping into an elder brother was nearly impossible.

I can hardly wait 'til it's done, Susan mused. The spacious new accommodations would have a cozy hearth, the hub of household togetherness, and maybe, eventually, one of those fancy new iron woodstoves that could be used for cooking not just to heat the house like the one they had now. She had already helped to plant a juniper tree in what would be their new front yard. Traditionally, it would bring renewed spirit to the family and the branches could be used to smoke the rooms free of all contagion and bad luck. Life changed so quickly sometimes that Susan could hardly keep pace.

As tedious as gardening duties could be, Susan loved the feel of the rich topsoil between her fingers and the shower of glowing yellow-green from new growth in the forested groves and fields that surrounded their family property. She knew that she should be grateful for the winter hours she had spent with Rebecca and their older siblings improving their skills in reading, writing, math and the religious instruction that filled the long evenings before the fire. Many girls she knew were limited to perfecting household skills and grooming themselves as prospective wives and mothers. Certainly the world of learning and books, even the few in their limited family library, was important, but the lure of the greening countryside made her ache to rejoin nature.

Though she knew she was needed in the kitchen, she dawdled by the tranquil yet swift rush of the creek, swollen with spring thaw. But as she daydreamed, she imagined less soothing visions at the forest edge on the not-too-distant horizon— visions of the once hostile Native Americans who nearly 50 years earlier might have hidden themselves from the young Renfrew sisters, Jane and Sarah, who were washing their family's clothes in the very stream that glittered in front of her.

Susan's father's voice had quavered as he told the tale of their horrible murder and scalping by hostile braves during the last days of the French and Indian War. Daniel Royer had been only two years old when the Renfrew girls were killed, but he recalled the story as vividly as when it was first told to him as a youngster. She often wondered if her father counted on this legend to discourage the wanderings of his more adventurous children. The bolder ones might be less apt to venture too far away from the safety of home if they thought of the awful fate of the Renfrew girls.

Susan tried to ignore her imaginings of the poor girls' screams of terror and preserve her blissful mood. Still, the violent images from the past sparked whisperings in the back of her mind of the disturbing remarks she was hearing from the adults about the threat of a 'new war' with the British that was brewing.

"Why can't everyone just get along?" she asked the early robin pecking at the softened earth on the opposite bank. He took flight in response as if to indicate he had no more answers than she.

Susan propped her head on her knees facing north to feel the shifting breeze brush her face and blow away her questions. Unfortunately, the air brought with it the unpleasant fumes of the large tannery operation nearby. Her father was a master of the trade and had passed his knowledge on to his eldest son David.

I don't know how they can stand the stink working there all day long sometimes, she thought.

Tanning was a long, arduous process to convert stiff, raw animal hides – mostly cowhides from neighboring farms – into soft leather for boots, clothing, leather sacks, and more. It took three other hardworking laborers employed by the family, along with the older brothers and Daniel, to run the operation. During the liming step, the animal skins soaked in large, wood-lined vats filled with caustic lime mixed with water diverted from the creek. This corrosive bath removed all of the flesh, fat and hair. After that, the skins fermented in another set of wood-lined vats layered with bark stripped from the stand of timber her father owned in the nearby forest. The hides were then dried and rubbed with oil and cured before they were ready for sale. It took two years to complete the process.

"Papa says that 'tanning's the only way to get everything from shoes to saddles and buckets to belts,' but it can certainly ruin a perfect day. Phew!"

Susan pointed her nose away from the tannery toward the gristmill and inhaled deeply. "Ahhh! The soapwort's already blooming around the mill." She closed her eyes and concentrated on the distant peaceful humming of the revolving millstones as they crushed the first of the season's grain.

The waterwheel of the new gristmill harnessed the energy of a small, man-made waterfall to run the gears. The stream-fed millpond beside the building and the millrace that ran in a ditch between the creek and the site of their new home had required many long hours of digging. Water from the pond above was released into the deep winding trench below. The waterfall channeled through the paddles of the waterwheel making it turn. The still pond attracted beautiful waterfowl and froze thick enough in winter to be cut into large blocks of ice that were stored in the far corner of the barn under layers of straw and burlap. The ice would last until summer when it would chill apple cider and ice the sweet cream laden with fresh peaches or berries.

Susan leaned against the grassy bank cradling the back of her head in her clasped hands and drank in the blue sky and skimming white puffs. Her mother would soon summon her to deliver the brimming oaken bucket and the watercress, but Susan would savor as much sweet reverie as she could until then.

-2-

REBECCA'S TRIP TO TOWN

"Rebecca, come on!" Samuel Royer shouted from his perch on the bench of the wagon outside the cabin. "It's time to go."

His spunky, seven-year-old sister pulled on her woolen modesty cape. She was so excited she could hardly tie the two ribbons near the collar and almost tripped over baby Nancy's cradle near the fireplace.

The youngest had been up all night with the croup keeping the entire household awake, but Catherine Royer, their Mama, had given her some tea made with dried catnip from the four-square garden, and she was sleeping peacefully enough now with a cloth soaked in linseed oil resting on her chest. Weak sunshine filtered through the narrow windows of their log house.

Mustn't wake her, Rebecca thought as she rushed to the door.

Today she and her older brother Samuel were heading to town to buy more redware crocks from Peter Bell's pottery. Bell offered the best crockery in the area, but his main shop was in  Hager's-town, Maryland – nearly a half day's trip from Waynesburg. Several times each year he loaded much of his stock and equipment into wagons and set up operations and sales on Market Days under large canvas tents in Waynesburg. All hands were needed at home this busy time of year, but Daniel had agreed to give up Samuel long enough to take advantage of Mr. Bell's visit. Mama had a real fondness for his work.

It was a short trip by wagon and Catherine told them they could not linger. The family needed more crocks for their hand-churned butter before the wagons left to deliver it to Frederick the next day. Much of the butter they had spent long hours churning over the past weeks would then make its way to the distant port of Baltimore where city residents gathering at the morning market would haggle over the cost of the farm-fresh staple. The Royer's sweet, creamy butter would fetch a high price there.

Samuel, wearing the cares of one older than his 20 years, waited impatiently for Rebecca to finally climb onto the wagon. She could tell he was anxious to get to town. She suspected that he was eager to catch a glimpse of Sarah Provines, the eldest daughter of the town's most prominent cooper. Her brother had obviously noticed Sarah with her golden hair tucked modestly under her small, white bonnet and her shy smile at last fall's Snitzen Party where everyone had gathered to string the dried apples and make apple butter and cider. Since that day, Samuel had quickly offered to take the wagon to town whenever Papa needed something, especially the well-crafted wooden barrels made by Sarah's father.

Rebecca gathered her skirts and thought, *Maybe something will happen between them today. I surely hope so.* Susan had told her that she was worried that their oldest brother David might take a shine to Sarah if Samuel waited much longer to court her. Samuel had said nothing about his interest in Sarah or his intentions as yet, still the girls couldn't help wondering.

"Let's go, Rebecca. The day is slipping away from us," Samuel said.

Taking Samuel's outstretched arm, Rebecca finally hopped onto the wagon bench beside him and smiled thinking, *Don't you let Sarah slip away, too.*

Samuel said little as he urged the horses onward. He hiked up the stiff, high collar of his plain homespun work shirt and she pulled her cloak a little tighter against a sudden breeze as the wagon lurched on the rutted pathway. The heady aroma of the spring air was a harbinger of the new growth of the season. The small buds would soon be wide oak leaves fluttering in the morning sunlight. She loved the newness in the air and the soft clopping of the horses' hooves on the damp path of dirt crumbling with the thaw. To her surprise Papa had allowed them to hitch up her favorite horses—sweet-tempered Elsie, the bay, and the brown mare, Tillie, who always nuzzled her looking for apple cores.

At the thought of apples, Rebecca's stomach started to growl in time with the rumble of the wagon. She had managed to eat only one Johnnycake dipped in maple syrup before they left, but she didn't mind. This rare occasion of release from household chores to ride to town next to her handsome brother made her sit up straighter and feel more grown up.

While passing the small Covenanters' cemetery at the eastern edge of their farm, Rebecca always crossed her fingers and held her breath for fear of distressed souls entering her body. She didn't know if the frightening tales of wandering spirits of the dead were true, but she wasn't taking any chances.

The timberline soon gave way to the sight of rooftops with smoke rising from chimneys and the faint sounds of commerce. Waynesburg was a cluster of two-dozen log, brick and weatherboard houses laid out on a grid. Masons were perched on scaffolding working on the White Swan as the brother and sister passed through the Center Square, a place known by everyone as "The Diamond." The tavern, whose second story was nearly complete, would be the first structure in town to be made entirely of stone.

The community with nearly 200 residents was named in honor of Revolutionary War General "Mad" Anthony Wayne and boasted several churches, a brewery, a log poorhouse, two cabinet makers, the carriage maker's shop and two cooperages. Rebecca heard the blacksmith's hammering and savored the smell of the fresh baked goods coming from her favorite place in town, the cake shop.

While Samuel negotiated a price with the potter, her job was to choose the crocks her mother needed from the rows of pottery inventory displayed on the temporary, heavy wooden planks in the large sales tent. Folks could tell the Bells were selling their wares that day because of the copper weathervane of a rooster placed high atop the center pole. The milk crocks, dishes, pitchers, jugs, bowls, and preserve jars came in a host of sizes. The Bell's pottery was artfully painted with flowers, birds or simple curlicues. Although Rebecca's older sisters and brothers laughed at her for saying so, she always believed that butter tasted sweeter when it came from a pretty crock. She could almost always distinguish pottery made by the Bell family from pieces made by the Bakers and other nearby potters. If ever she had any doubt, all she had to do was turn the piece over. The proud Bell potters always stamped their names into the base of their handiwork before placing the shaped clay objects into the kiln where the heat of the slow-burning wood fire miraculously turned what came from the earth into useful household items.

Mr. Bell fashioned practical, everyday items from the rich red clay dug from pits abundant in the area. In the smaller tent behind the sales area, the artisans sat at their humming potter's wheels working their artistic magic. On a trip the previous spring with her father, Rebecca had observed the spinning of the potter's wheel and was mesmerized by its insistent whirr and the seamless transformation of a misshapen ball of wet clay into a perfectly symmetrical urn, bowl or tankard. The potter was not troubled by the slithering clay coating his hands. Lulled by the rhythm of the wheel before him, he was lost in the act of creation.

Could this have been how God made man in the very beginning? she recalled wondering.

Rebecca drew from her list of memorized Bible verses. *How did that one go – the one from Genesis? . . . a stream would rise from the earth . . . then the Lord God formed man from the dust of the ground . . .*

She couldn't resist slipping back to the work tent to watch the process after she made her selections, leaving Samuel to complete the transaction. Today, just as then, she wanted terribly to try her hand at the wheel, even knowing how Mama would scold her if she got the sticky clay on her sleeves and skirt. Still, a more practical voice in her mind always prevailed. *What am I possibly thinking? After all, only men can be potters. Working with clay is an unseemly occupation for a young lady.*

But withal, she couldn't help but envy what she imagined must be the thrill of feeling the moist earth take on such lovely shapes in her hands. So lost was she in watching the clattering wheel revolve again today that Samuel called three times before she answered. Only at the last bark was she aware of the sharpness of his tone, still not nearly as frightening as their oldest brother, David, who was much more like their stern father.

"Rebecca! Stop dawdling," Samuel insisted when he finally got her attention. "The crocks are nearly loaded and we have to stop at the cooperage for Papa before we start home!"

Rebecca quickly remembered Sarah Provinces who waited at the cooper's shop and dashed to the family wagon. As she passed the side of one of the potter's freight wagons, John Bell, the potter's youngest son – not much older than Rebecca herself – hooked his thumbs around his suspenders and peeked from behind one of the sturdy oaken wheels. He smiled sympathetically noticing Rebecca's anxiety at her brother's commands. He remembered her fascination with the working potters and her pretty smile from the last time she had visited the tent.

Rebecca's parents and others often remarked on the backwardness of the master potter's sons and assistants. 'Never marry a potter,' Mrs. McBride, their bossy neighbor, said one day over hot cider on one of her many unexpected visits. 'They make plenty of pots all right, but they never have one of their own to pee in. Besides, they're all *ferhoodled*, as you Germans say – you know, a little crazy in the head, maybe from all the lead in the glazes. Poison stuff that is!' she had declared shaking her finger at them.

When all of the crocks were safely cushioned in wicker baskets full of sawdust and fresh straw in the wagon, Samuel went into the shop to pay Mr. Bell with the bushel of corn and jars of honey they had brought. Nearly all of their commercial transactions involved bartering goods and services. Hard currency in the form of silver pieces and gold coins was scarce.

While Samuel was distracted, John motioned to Rebecca. Sensing a hint of conspiracy in John's manner, Rebecca, ever the curious one, looked over her shoulder and when she realized no one was paying attention to them, she ventured nearer. He pulled a small object from his pocket. "Here, take this. It's for you."

Rebecca couldn't believe her eyes. In his palm rested a little, red clay bird with a small spout for a tail. Its little open beak was ready to break out in song. She knew what it was instantly. Her very own bird whistle! John lowered his head and blushed as she took it into her small hands. Before she could say anything, Samuel scooped her up and plopped her onto the wagon bench. They were halfway down the town's dirt road heading toward the cooper's shop before she could finally turn around and safely wave a thank you to John in the distance.

Rebecca didn't mind when Samuel asked her to stay with the wagon while he went to see Mr. Provines. After all, she had her new whistle to entertain her and a perfect bird's-eye view to observe Sarah Provines in front of the shop and discover what might transpire between her and Samuel. From what Rebecca could see, the pretty Miss Provines was sweeping the clean-smelling wood shavings from the porch – boards that had already been swept clean – just so she could hover close enough to hear Samuel's conversation with her father. They were talking barrel sizes. The Royers would need six new hogsheads and two small wooden pails for hauling water.

Samuel talked as Mr. Provines listened patiently. Rebecca's pulse quickened when she noticed Sarah sending timid glances Samuel's way, but rather than stare at the two of them, Rebecca focused on her little clay treasure. Still, she couldn't help but notice Samuel tip the brim of his hat and nod in Sarah's direction just before he boarded the wagon. He then managed a tender smile at Sarah who eagerly returned the small overture with a giggle – but that was all.

Later when Samuel stopped to pay the four-cent toll at the tollgate outside of town, Rebecca hid under the hood of her cape, put the tiny whistle to her mouth and blew air through the spout, making the quietest sound she could. Luckily Samuel didn't notice. Mama and Papa didn't approve of calling attention to oneself. They surely would not approve of something as showy as a whistle, or the fact that she had accepted a gift from the young John Bell. This would have to stay her secret. She couldn't wait to slip into the woods and discover just how big a sound this little clay bird could make. For now, safely hidden in her waist pocket, Rebecca ran her fingers over its smooth, glazed surface all the way home. Maybe she would tell her older sister and best friend Susan, but no one else.

"You're the quiet one today," said Samuel noticing how subdued his sister had become. She was the one always brimming with energy, chattering like a flock of sparrows. Over the creak of the wagon wheels he asked, "Cat got your tongue?"

"No." Rebecca said. Then she thought to herself. *More like a little birdie.* She went on, "But, I must say, Samuel, it seemed as though *you* swallowed *your* tongue when you should have wiggled it a little more."

"Is that so?" said Samuel.

"Actually, I'd say that Sarah Provines was wanting to hear the sound of your voice today."

Samuel smiled at the puffing horses pulling the wagon up the slight incline.

"Really?" He blushed, but dared not look at her.

"Really!" she insisted. "David would have noticed Sarah's giggle and started up a conversation for sure . . . and he might be the one who's sent to get the next batch of barrels."

Samuel said nothing the rest of the trip, his smile lost to more serious musings. Rebecca, even at seven, knew she had said enough.

-3-

DAILY LIFE

"**S**usan!" Her mother's summons tumbled down to the streamside. "Susan?"

Try as she might, Susan couldn't answer immediately. She already knew why she was wanted. In addition to the watercress and the full bucket of water her mother had asked her to fetch, it was her week to churn the butter. As delicious as it tasted on Mama's newly-baked biscuits or fresh roastin' ears, Susan's arms ached just at the thought of pumping those baffles again and again until the butter formed up enough from the milk to press it into molds for the dinner table.

Her 14-year-old brother, John, milked Reba and Bessie, the family's two Shorthorn milk cows, every day before sunup.

 What wasn't poured onto the bowls of breakfast mush or needed later in the day was destined for the wooden churn. Completing the transformation of the milky liquid into creamy butter was a never-ending chore. Whatever extra butter they had

accumulated in the milk house would go to market when Papa made his monthly delivery to Frederick. The green grasses of May through September made for the sweetest butter, but the task of churning knew no season. Hours working the baffles of the churn up and down always made her fingers stiff and her arms ache.

"Susan Royer, milk jugs are waitin' in the milk house and none of us are gettin' any younger here." Catherine Royer planted her hands on her ample hips and scanned the horizon for her absent daughter.

"Coming, Mama!" Susan shouted over her shoulder toward the log cabin. She pushed herself up with her open palms from the cushiony bank and headed for home.

At least I'll have first try at the cool buttermilk, she told herself unable to resist smiling at the prospect.

As she trudged up the slope with the sloshing bucket and apron full of watercress, she heard the clatter of the family wagon returning from town. She turned to see Rebecca seated alongside Samuel on the seat. *Looks like it was a quick trip today*, she thought. *Hope next time – when it's my turn to go, we can stay longer. Wonder if Rebecca has any news about Samuel and Sarah.* But Rebecca jumped from the wagon and disappeared through the cabin door before Susan could get her attention.

"There you are," scolded Mama spotting Susan. "Thought you might have gotten tangled in the watercress and fallen in the stream."

"Sorry, Mama. I just *had* to stop a minute and take in this beautiful day."

"Well, I just *have* to have some beautiful butter before noon meal, too. But, maybe I can help you combine those two necessities a little."

Nearly an hour later, Susan licked the eggshell-colored mustache of rich buttermilk from her upper lip as she gazed with satisfaction at the large crockery bowl laden with hunks of fresh creamy butter. At Mama's request, 12-year-old brother Jacob had moved the wooden churn to the cabin's front porch, a pleasant arrangement for Susan on such a sparkling spring day. Mukki, the family's spaniel mix was stretched out under the rough-hewn porch bench, the golden feathers of her long tail spreading across the sanded boards. Susan was lost again in the sailing clouds as she massaged the tightness from her biceps, when Rebecca came flying around the side of the chicken house.

She's such a sprite, thought Susan. *Always dashing here and there*. But as her little sister sped past the front door, she paused just long enough to offer, "Papa's coming, Susan. Best

stay out of his way – he's got the look of the devil in his eye."
She disappeared around the far corner of the barn.

The dust from Rebecca's retreat had barely settled when
Daniel Royer's intense stride kicked up new clouds with each
pounding step as he marched his staunch frame toward the
house. His ruddy, leathered face showed even more crimson in
contrast to the dusting of white flour that powdered his grizzled
beard and damp, dark hair and clung to the sweat of his sinewy
forearms and rough-nap of his work clothes. He was a hard man
– in body and in spirit – and well his family knew that. His
strength was their bulwark against all of the unnamed hardships
that might threaten them, but his harsh discipline allowed little
room for compassion or patience.

Susan shrank into the wooden bench as much as
possible hoping to avoid her father's obvious anger. She eased
slightly as he pushed open the front door, but he stopped short
before crossing the threshold and groused without even turning
his head toward her. "Get that butter out of the sun before it
turns. Waste not – want not. Now move!" Mukki slinked out
from under the bench and followed Rebecca's earlier path to the
barn.

"Yes, Papa." But Susan's response fell
on empty air as the door slapped shut behind
him. She glanced at the *Hexefuss* carved in the
flat–hewn section of log just above the

entrance to the cabin and said a silent prayer that the five-pointed star live up to its power to keep any evil spirits from sweeping in behind him.

Mama will have all she can handle with just Papa alone, she thought. She wiped her hands on her work apron and gathered the slippery bowl carefully to her chest.

Dare not drop it with Papa in such a mood, she warned herself. *Probably best to store it in the milk house for now. I'll move the churn back inside later when I won't disturb whatever is causing all of this ruckus.*

Daniel tore off his frosted, wide-brimmed hat, an ever-present sign of his German Baptist reverence to God, and planted it on the peg just inside the door of the log house. His 50 years of living had known little else but work. A true man's worth was measured by his faith, his strength, his resolve to succeed, and the security he could provide for his family. His wife and children would worship God, labor hard, and obey him without question. For his part, he would protect them, work without ceasing to provide the best life possible for them, and pray daily for God's blessing and guidance.

Daniel's dedication to these ends made him a formidable figure and an often unwelcome adversary. His frequent scowls prompted those around him to quickly remedy whatever caused his displeasure. A man of few words, he expected his family to ascertain by mere observation what they needed to do to soften his expression. Was it more salt to the stew, prompter milking of the family cow, less chatter at the table? Reading his mind in order to react promptly and properly challenged Susan and her siblings more often than they liked. Their mother had more experience with Daniel's unspoken requests. She had mastered a long look that she directed at her husband at such times that calmed him without challenging his authority.

On occasions when Daniel inflicted both his bark and bite on one of them, Susan had to hold fast to the rare glimpses of his softer side that he had let slip. These memories helped her to preserve a loving respect for her father in spite of his usual callous reactions. She remembered how he had paced the floor for hours on end months earlier when her sister Nancy refused to be easily born – how he had winced with each of her mother's cries all night long. The other children had gone along with 16-year-old sister Polly to the neighbors while Catherine gave birth leaving just her older sister, 18-year-old Elizabeth, and Susan to help the midwife with the hot water and cool cloths and to tend to all the other household tasks. She still recalled the glow of unconditional love on Daniel's face when he sat beside his exhausted wife and newborn Nancy. Susan somehow knew that this was the father who was present at each of their births—who loved them and would never let anything hurt them, or his beloved Catherine.

She recalled how her father had agonized over her brother's pain when the doctor set the leg that John snapped when he jumped from the hayloft to retrieve a bale that had accidentally fallen. How Papa had celebrated when her sister Cate, now five years old, took her first steps. She marveled at the serenity that sometimes washed over him during prayers. But, this wasn't today's Daniel who was ranting to her mother, his harsh words echoing from the other side of the wall.

I wonder what has him so upset, she thought as she shoved the churn back against the wall with her feet. *I can't leave this in his way, for sure.* She made her way behind the cabin toward the milk house that was cooled by running water diverted from the stream. *It must have been something that happened at the mill. He was still covered with flour when he passed me – and he usually dusts most of it off before he comes home.*

She stowed the crock of butter covered with a fine homespun cloth in the milk house and quickly closed the heavy, wooden door behind her to preserve the natural coolness.

She thought out loud, "David might have been at the mill with him. Maybe I'll get a chance to ask him tonight." She frowned. "Not that he'll tell me. He's gotten so high and mighty lately – like he's so much better than the rest of us. Seems that older he gets, the nastier he gets. I can hear him now, 'Why would I tell you? You're just a girl; now go fetch some water or something. Make yourself useful and mind your own business.' She flopped to the ground and leaned back against the apple tree. "Well, if it's his business, then it can be my business, too."

Just then she caught a glimpse of Rebecca through the open barn door scurrying around the side of Elsie's stall. *Maybe she heard something before she ran away*, Susan hoped as she scrambled to her feet and headed for her sister's retreat in the hay. *Besides, I need to ask her if anything exciting happened in town today.*

- 4-

DANIEL'S ANGER

Catherine kept a steady rhythm chopping carrots for the midday meal as Daniel stormed in and paced the packed dirt floor of the cabin. When she finally heard the chair pulled from the table and Daniel's breathing become steadier as he settled against the curved slats of the chair back, she calmly moved to the sink basin, took down the largest tin cup hanging on the wall and worked the pump handle until it drew cool water. She added a splash of cider, placed the full cup on the table in front of Daniel, sat down on the bench to his right and waited silently. Without prompting, Polly took Cate's hand and followed Elizabeth who had plucked Nancy from the cradle. They slipped out the back door to give their parents some privacy.

Daniel took a long draft of water and leaned forward over the nearly empty cup, his elbows on the table and his hands clasped under his tight mouth. "He challenges me, Catherine. He tries my righteousness. Preaching my own doctrine to me, he was, like I was a school child. Tellin' me his good conscience wouldn't let him pay the taxes he owes – saying the Lord calls us to be separate of the law. 'The law' he says to me as if paying his fair share for the good of the community is a sin. How dare him!" Daniel pounded the table with his fist spilling what remained of his drink.

Catherine softly laid her hand on Daniel's wrist above his clenched fist. "Who, Daniel?"

He looked up from under his heavy, furrowed eyebrows. "Jonas Lehman, from over by the marsh. That self-righteous scoundrel defied me – chastised me – in front of Amos and my customers – in front of my son. As much as branded me a sinner, he did." He threw himself back into the chair. "I tell you, Catherine, it was all I could do to keep a civil tongue in my head – to keep fair-dealing grain and milling with him, and him blaspheming me like he was!"

Daniel pushed up from the chair and crossed to the open hearth. He stared into the smoldering fire. "I nearly struck him, Catherine. I felt my arm tighten around the neck of a flour bag to heave across his back. I swear to you, Catherine, it must have been the hand of the Lord Himself who kept that sack on the mill floor. David hustled him out of there before I lost control.

Catherine rose and turned to him, but kept a distance respectful of his authority and his anger. People know you are a good man, Daniel – godly man. They know the magistrate appointed you to the job as tax collector. You didn't ask for it, but you accepted the responsibility. The community of believers respects and trusts you. It's not a popular job you have, Husband. It takes a man of your strength to do it. Those such as Jonas Lehman, who see our doctrine differently, who tend to put themselves above us, will be your cross to bear. Our Lord has and will continue to help you."

As Daniel turned to respond, David burst in the front door. "*Vater!* ... "

Catherine raised her palm to her son to silence him. "The news has already been told David. It was a regretful thing that happened, but we are dealing with it best we can."

David looked to his father for confirmation, but Daniel felt his son's eyes on him and avoided his inquiring stare as he stirred the embers with the iron poker. "What do you mean to do, Father? You can't let ... "

Catherine saw Daniel's eyes widen. She stepped toward her firstborn and touched his sleeve. "As I said, David, it was an awful thing, but don't presume to tell your father what he can or cannot do. Mr. Lehman will be dealt with as he chooses, not us."

"You don't understand, Mama. Mr. Lehman can't ... "

The clang of the iron poker dropping hard against the hearth cut him off. "Did you not hear your mother, David?" Daniel asked flatly with his jaw still set. "Best we get on down to the tannery and work out some of this righteous anger in honest labor. Those hides aren't going to shave themselves, you know. Who's helping Mr. Fahnestock at the mill, son?"

"I called Samuel in from repairing the barn shingles. He can handle what's left of the trade today."

"Good, he'll bring some calm to the air there, for sure. Not a bad thing – not a bad thing at all. The Lord gives each of us gifts of His choosing. I fear, David, you have inherited my temper, very handy in some instances, but more often than not, in need of better control than we can muster, it seems."

Catherine added a silent Amen to her husband's pronouncement. "Bread's not going to bake itself while we stand here either. The day is nearly half gone already and no one will enjoy dinner as much with no way to sop up the gravy. David, be sure to tote some cider down to the tannery. I'm sure George and the other men have worked up a sweat with the new spring heat. Mind you and your Papa drink plenty yourselves." She handed him the large tin pitcher from the sideboard.

With a tone of normalcy restored, the men gave each other a confirming look and proceeded out the door. Catherine sighed in relief as she made her way to the rear door to retrieve her daughters.

"Girls, you can come back in here and lend a hand," she directed as she lifted the wooden latch. They filed back into the cabin and resumed their tasks without a word. Elizabeth returned Nancy to the cradle and began to scoop some dried corn into a bowl as Polly instructed Cate in helping prepare the table for the noon meal.

Catherine wiped her hands on her work apron before attacking the yeast-inflated dough peeking out from under the cloth covering the large spatterwear bowls on the table. One last kneading was necessary before forming it into loaves and beginning the baking process to stock the week's larder. Just as she buried her fist in the first mound of risen dough, baby Nancy's soft murmurs bubbled over into a more insistent whimper. Catherine knew that she had only a minute before her babe would insist on being fed. The instinctive motherly reaction dampened the bib of her apron and she smiled to herself. "Be right there, *mein Kindlein*. I'm nearly finished here." *Thank goodness she's got my patience and not Daniel's*, Catherine thought as she deftly wrestled the dough, formed it into the first loaves and popped them into the small, brick baking oven at the side of the hearth.

Moments later mother and child moved together gently in the rocking chair bathed in sunlight and serenity in the middle of their busy world as Catherine softly sang:

34

Schlaf, leibling, schlaf!
Der Vater Hut't die Schaf.
Die Mutter schuttelt's Baumelein,
Da Fallt herab ein Traumelein.
Schlaf, Kindlein, schlaf!

Sleep, darling. sleep
Father tends the sheep.
Mother shakes the little tree,
From which falls a little dream.
Sleep, child, sleep.

-5-

SUSAN AND REBECCA

Heavy silence stretched from the wide oak beams to the straw-strewn dirt floor of the Royer's modest barn. All of the stalls stood empty. *Jacob's been busy*, thought Susan scanning for some sign of Rebecca. The cows were grazing in the pasture after their morning milking and the plow mule was pulling 14-year-old brother John, who guided the rod iron-tipped plow turning up furrows in the warming spring soil. More stubborn farmers believed that the rod iron poisoned the soil and still used only wooden-tipped plows. John was thankful his papa was more progressive as his straining biceps battled the formidable crusts of earth.

By the barn, Elsie and Tillie shook their manes and hung their heads in the water trough with their glossy chestnut coats soaking up the sun.

"Rebecca?" called Susan. No response. "Rebecca?" It was too quiet. Susan smiled and alerted all of her senses for a clue. A tumble of hay from behind the wooden barricade of

Tillie's stall near the middle of the building caught her eye. A calico kitten pounced from hiding at the movement as if attacking an invading mouse. Rebecca's small hand crawled from the same spot and snatched a tiny paw. As she dragged the kitten back out of view, a shrill meow signaled the end of this game of hide-and-seek.

Susan made her way around the end of the stall. She slid down beside her sister and scooped up one of the calico's littermates and stroked her finger gently under the feathery, cotton ball chin, marveling at the brown, black and golden fur swirled through a background of white. Susan leaned into Rebecca and over the purring bunch of fur in her hand she asked, "Sister, what happened at the mill today? Father nearly ripped the door from its hinges when he came home. Did you hear or see anything that might make him so *gretzy*?"

Rebecca straightened her back and squared her shoulders feeling the power of secret knowledge. Then she peeked around the end of the stall to make sure no unwelcome eavesdroppers had joined them. "Oh Susan, it was *shrecklich*. I never saw Papa so angry as he was today. If you ask me—and you are asking me – Mr. Lehman was lucky to leave with his head."

"Why? What did Mr. Lehman do to anger Papa so?"

"Papa and David, too." Rebecca tightened her lips and shook her head. "It was mostly grown-up talk I heard. I was just outside the mill door sitting on the bank making a flower chain from the soapwort patch when the ruckus began. Something about 'taxes' and 'fair share' – and Mr. Lehman said something about Papa 'had no right.' David stepped in and finished up business with Mr. Lehman. Then it was stone quiet until Mr. Lehman was out of earshot and David said, 'Good riddance to such as them that think they are better than others.' That set Papa off again. He stomped out of the mill door and nearly tripped over my basket of dandelion greens that Mama told me to collect for dinner."

"I suppose the best way for us is to stay quiet and do as Papa says. Mama will tell us what we need to know, and maybe we can find a time to ask her to explain what happened when Papa and David aren't around," Susan said.

Rebecca laid the calico kitten in her muslin apron and rocked it gently in the makeshift cradle. "Sometimes I wish I could make myself disappear when Papa loses his temper. His eyes look like the McBride's bull when we get too close." The tempo of her swinging apron increased. "Remember last harvest season – Jacob's pumpkin?"

Susan recalled vividly the smashed jack-o-lantern, a Scotch-Irish seasonal tradition and gift to their 12-year-old brother from neighbor Mrs. McBride for his help stacking hay bales after her husband, Silas, twisted his back. When Daniel had returned from the fields exhausted and saw the carved pumpkin by the front door, he fairly exploded and flung it at the first thing he saw – an unsuspecting Mukki who was asleep under the porch bench. The dog barely escaped the impact, but Jacob carried his welts for nearly a week – 'signs of the same Devil as carves pumpkins,' according to his father.

"Yes," she told Rebecca, "I remember it was a bad time all around. Papa had been working so hard that day and Jacob knew no better—either that *Mr.* McBride had challenged Papa earlier that week about milling costs *or* that *Mrs.* McBride's gift was an 'abomination to God.'

"I know, Sister, but poor Mukki had nothin' in it."

"Which is why it's always best to give Papa his space when he's vexed. Even more so now with so much talk of another war with those awlful British Redcoats. Both Opah Royer and Opah Stoner served during the Revolutionary War all those years ago, and Papa, who was no older than David, herded cattle all the way to Valley Forge to feed General Washington's starving troops. Even though we won our independence from the British back then, they've come back – and too close for comfort. Their huge ships are blockading the port in Baltimore. Everyone is so worried and scared. It's good to know Papa could handle them just like he did that carved pumpkin, isn't it?" Susan replied in defense of her father's occasional rage.

"I guess so," Rebecca acknowledged hesitantly. She picked stray bits of straw from the laces of her well-worn shoes, once Susan's and before her Polly's. The leather, cured and treated in the Royer family tannery, had worn like iron. Soon the weather would allow the children the freedom of bare feet and thick calluses on their soles.

The kittens began chasing some pesky flies close by, but Rebecca didn't pursue them this time. These complex adult motivations that Susan spoke of were heady musings, especially for a seven-year-old.

Susan sensed her sister's misgivings. She didn't always understand their father's outbursts herself, but needed to appear a wise confidante to Rebecca. Not only were they children, but girl children – to be seen and not heard. Observation and deduction were their most reliable tools – sometimes enhanced by their mother's feedback. As Rebecca's older sister, Susan's role was to share the more extensive experience that her two extra years of life granted her. Polly, her older sister by nine years, had been her mentor about such matters before, and Susan longed to match the comforting example she had set.

"I guess it's not easy being a grown-up sometimes, especially when you are as important a man in the community as Papa is. They have so much to think about – so many decisions to make every day. And now with little Nan, there are ten of us to take care of, not counting Mama and Papa, plus all of the folk who work in the tannery and the mill. We must be as obedient and helpful as we can, even if everything he does doesn't always make sense."

"I try, Susan. Really I do," said Rebecca. "I want to do what's right, but sometimes I can't figure out what that is." She looked around the end of the stall again for any uninvited guests and then leaned into Susan and continued in hushed tones. "Like with the Lehmans. Mr. Lehman upsets Papa so, but his son Edward is so nice and kind – like the time he shushed Sean McBride for making fun of Jacob's hat and your bonnet even though Sean is bigger and older than he is. And just last week, Edward offered me part of his meal at Sunday meeting when he saw me drop my butter-bread onto the dirt floor. Is it all right to be friends with him even though Papa is so angry with Mr. Lehman?"

Susan laid her arm on Rebecca's shoulder. "I don't think you can blame the son for what the father does. What Edward did was good and he can't control his papa's actions any more than we can control our Papa's. It's fine to be friendly to Edward whenever you see him, just don't be going to his house to play with his little sister, Ruth, so you won't have to deal with Mr. Lehman directly. That makes sense, doesn't it?"

Rebecca smiled. "Well, it makes me feel better, anyway."

"At least that's the way I see it. I mean, Mrs. Lehman always notices the best things about our four-square garden.

When she tells me how pretty it looks, I see no harm in offering her one of our ripe summer squash or some of Mama's bright dahlias for her windowsill. I don't think Papa would mind at all, and Mama's face always welcomes Mrs. Lehman when she comes over for spinning or canning and such. I'm sure she wouldn't do that if we should be avoiding the whole of the Lehman family."

The mention of ripe squash set Rebecca's mouth watering. The noon-high sun ignited sparks on the smooth surface of the water in the horse trough and confirmed the approach of the midday dinner—always the most ample meal of the day.

"I say, let's go help Mama with dinner chores," chimed Rebecca. She hopped up and set her hands firmly on her hips. "And I say, that when I mentioned Edward Lehman's name your eyes lit up like they do at Mama's hot apple pie – at something sweet," she teased.

Susan swallowed a smile as her hand closed on a fistful of hay. She flung it at her sister. "That's how much you know, Rebecca." Following her hasty retreat to the house, she added, "Wait up, Rebecca. You still didn't tell me what happened in town today."

As they burst through the front door, their mother nearly dropped the bundle of hot bread bound for the table. "Well," she said, "looks like spring fever has you two in quite a twitter.

Harness some of that energy and help me. Susan, fill the pitcher and Rebecca ring the dinner bell. I'm sure everybody's hungry by now."

-6-

THE NOON MEAL

"Where's Jacob?" Catherine asked John, who, like the rest of her clan, was standing behind his seat at the table. No one would be seated until enough were present for Papa to ask the blessing. She had certainly consulted the appropriate source about her son's absence since the two brothers, 12 and 14, were usually inseparable.

John shrugged. "He was plowing the far cornfield last I saw him, Mama."

Although Daniel remained uncharacteristically patient, Catherine shook her head. "The food's getting cold and losing its flavor. I wonder . . ." She glanced out the window.

David clenched his fists at the inconvenience caused by his younger brother. A delay in the family meal meant a delay in the food his mother would serve right afterward to the three tannery workers and two carpenters working on the new family home. Only the miller, Amos Fahnestock, whose family lived in a small house nearby, provided a noon meal for himself. *Time is money*, David brooded silently, *and I prefer to waste neither—Zeit ist Geld*. Samuel sensed his older brother's impatience and glanced at him sympathetically trying to calm him and preserve peace at the meal. David caught the look, but would have none of it. He had little respect for Samuel's softness, as he saw it.

Jacob bounded in the door, shirtsleeves rolled to the elbows and covered in mud. "Sorry I'm late. Just as the dinner bell rang the mule jerked hard right and got stuck in a muddy swale near the split rail. Had to get him out and tied up before I could come."

"Come to table first so Papa can offer the blessing and these hungry children don't starve. Then wash up before you eat," Catherine said.

Jacob promptly complied as he moved behind the long side bench to his regular dinner seat beside his elder, curly-haired brother John. They often worked side-by-side in the fields and with the daily upkeep of the animals and heavy necessities of house and barn, but today their chores  had kept them apart. John's hands were etched with cross-hatchings from his encounter with the splintered rails of the fences he had been repairing that morning as Jacob plowed. John poked Jacob with his elbow and they both grinned as the entire family faced one another across the table.

"What foolery," David grumbled.

"That is quite enough, David,"said Catherine positioning herself at the end of the table opposite a distracted Daniel. Everyone waited, all eyes on their father who remained stark and oblivious. Catherine coughed gently, then a bit louder to jar him to the present.

He looked at her puzzled. "The blessing, Daniel," she reminded him.

"Oh, yes, of course." He clasped his hands together in front of his chest and closed his eyes. The rest of the table followed suit, but waited in awkward silence.

After a pause Daniel opened his eyes and spoke, "I find it difficult to offer proper thanks just now. That German Baptist, as he calls himself, has sorely tried my Christian patience." He dropped his hands as his voice tightened. "The utter gall of him to . . ."

"I hope the venison is seasoned to your liking, Daniel," Catherine fairly yelled hoping to head off such upset in front of the children.

Daniel's irritation was obvious, but he quieted quickly as he understood her reaction and recalled his own earlier self-recrimination about his temper. He paused and then nodded to

Elizabeth, his eldest daughter, 21 years of age, and the most spiritual of his children. "Elizabeth, if you wouldn't mind."

Everyone at the table turned to her. Elizabeth's ever-present sense of calm and reverence tempered the anger in the air. She was the picture of piety. Her dark brown hair was parted in the middle and drawn tightly into a modest bun—her solemn face molded by serenity, rarely betrayed any emotion—her posture softly erect as if in a constant state of grace.

"Of course, Papa," she answered as everyone resumed their prayerful attitude. "Our heavenly Father, bless this food and . . ."

After the family's communal Amen, David was the first to take his seat and attack his ample serving of venison stew, sauerkraut, and biscuits. As he dipped his fingers into the saltcellar in the center of the table carelessly scattering a trail of it to his plate, Susan caught her breath hoping he would take the time to toss a few grains over his left shoulder. It was likely he wouldn't because for him, despite the risk of bad luck to follow, the undue expense of the salt would stop him. Salt was a precious commodity. Not only was it used to flavor meals, it was essential for preserving many perishable foods. The family's supply of salt was hauled by pack team from Baltimore only twice a year. However, the last time Susan had ignored this rite regarding spilled salt, she caught her apron on the barberry bush twice within the day. She knew some folks thought it was a silly superstition, but she wasn't convinced.

Better safe than sorry, she thought. *I'd remind him, but he would never listen to me.* As she suspected, David, who would take directions from none but his father, simply continued eating after a mumbled apology for the salt he had spilled in his haste.

As the last slice of bread disappeared from the cutting board, Daniel pushed his empty plate toward the middle of the long, oak table. The subdued tone of the meal had continued with the children's tentative glances at their father anticipating some indication of when, and if, the solemnity could pass and allow for more relaxed conversation. Catherine was thankful for her children's caution. They knew Daniel's moods quite well and how to accommodate them.

When Daniel became unsettled by the extended silence, he pivoted his chair toward the front windows. The tautness in his shoulders relaxed as he drew in a deep breath and slowly released it. "Seems to me that the day's not going to wait for us. There is plenty of work waiting for everyone while the sun still shines. The Lord has given us a fine day for our labors." He looked squarely at Catherine, but delivered the directive to all. "Does anyone lack for something productive to do now that our bellies are full?"

A sprinkling of "No, Papas" from the children peppered the bits of food that remained on the table. Only Rebecca faltered.

"Do you have a concern, Rebecca?" he asked noticing her hesitation.

"I . . . I . . . ," she stammered

"She can help me break dirt in the four-square garden for the spring vegetables," Susan said sensing Rebecca's dilemma.

Satisfied with the suggestion, Daniel stood up. "*Gut*, no idle hands then. Let's get to what needs done this day."

-7-

THE FOUR-SQUARE GARDEN

The Royer family's four-square garden, as those of the many of the local German families, was an invaluable source for most of the household needs providing nearly all of the family's vegetables, herbs,  medicines and even some occasional decorative flowers. The neatness of the rows and the tidiness of the beds showed any with eyes to see how well the *Frau* cared for her family. Sensing her instinctive connection with the soil and her pleasure in the process, Catherine had recently entrusted Susan with much of the work formerly done by 16-year-old Polly. This reassignment pleased both the girls and their mother as it freed Polly to help Catherine with the serving of noon meal to the hired help and put Susan in charge of the garden. Also, Susan noticed what her mother, it seemed, had missed with her preoccupation with her many labors. One of the tannery workers, burly young George Schmucker, was usually awarded the largest slice of apple pandowdy or rhubarb pie when Polly was serving – not to mention the flush in both of their cheeks when she passed close to him. Just last Wednesday's noon meal, Susan was sure she saw Polly slip something into the small pocket sewn to the inside of her waistband right after she served George his portion of *shnitz un knep.*

Polly was full of life. Her thick, brown curls fought daily to escape from under her cap and her chestnut eyes held a constant spark of mischief. She welcomed industrious tasks that matched her natural strength. If not delicate, she was endearing and solidly beautiful. The limits set by her family's German Baptist faith and life's rules in general troubled her more than they did her brothers and sisters.

Now no one could argue that George Schmucker was a fine figure of a young man causing many of the village girls to swoon. He was unaffected, perhaps even unaware of his effect on girls, but *quite* sure of his feelings for Polly with her ready laugh and hearty spirit. When his smiles fell on her, she couldn't help but respond in kind although she knew it would not please her parents, especially Daniel. Although George was of their religion, recent dissention among the congregation might make that more of a hindrance than a help. Just such differences in belief had caused much of the trouble at the mill earlier that day. Also, George was not very secure in his financial future being the youngest of four sons from a family holding barely 20 acres of land. Still, he was one of their best workers and actually got along with David, in spite of his sometimes harsh treatment of the tannery workers.

Susan and Rebecca placed their sunbonnets over their small white caps for the first time this growing season and proceeded to the shed at the inside corner of their small barn to arm themselves with the necessary tools for their gardening labors as agreed upon at the noon meal. A sturdy, whitewashed picket fence bordered in season by flowers and medicinal plants surrounded the traditional 66-by-66-foot square of ground located near the house. Inside the fence, four smaller square-shaped corner beds, bordered by paths and filled with rows of vegetables, surrounded the center to make up the larger square. The beds were raised and enclosed by wooden planks to allow for warmth, drainage and ease of weeding and harvesting.

"Here, you carry these," said Susan handing Rebecca a digging trowel and small iron hand rake. "And don't run with them," she cautioned relishing the role of supervisor.

"All right, Susan." Rebecca carefully folded them into her work apron anxious to live up to her new responsibilities and her sister's expectations. After their mother had taught the eldest, Elizabeth, about the four-square garden, each of the succeeding sisters passed this knowledge to the next sister in line – Elizabeth to Polly to Susan – and so on to Rebecca. In a few short years, Rebecca would teach little Cate who would finally pass the information on to baby Nan. Rebecca realized full well that she must be a good student to continue this important tradition.

Cooking fat applied liberally to the sharp edges and points of the implements had kept them free of winter rust and eased the friction of digging in the crusted soil. As with many of the garden activities, the 'greasing' was associated with the family's religion. On Shrove Tuesday, the last day before Lent, the family feasted on Catherine's homemade *Faschtnachts*. Leftover fat from frying the sweet doughnuts was used to oil the tools. Faschtnacht Day was the last day that they would have sweets until Easter morning.

On Ash Wednesday, immediately following Faschtnacht Day, they spread the idle garden beds with ashes from the fireplace. This, mixed with the manure they had added periodically during warmer winter days, helped to fertilize the well-used soil.

On this early spring day, the girls inspected the perennial medicinal plants and some cooking herbs, such as sage and meadowsweet that had broken ground around the garden gate weeks earlier. The hops vines were beginning to work their way up the stakes along the inside of the picket fence to their left. That harvest would yield the necessary yeast for the endless breads and cakes it took to keep the family satisfied.

Susan unlatched the gate for Rebecca and made certain to secure it after they entered. A stray cow or sheep, even a rabbit, groundhog or the occasional white-tailed deer, could do significant damage if they got in.

"We'll start on this half of the northwest square," she said pointing to the appropriate plot.

"Look," said Rebecca, "the potatoes and peas in the other half are already pushing up shoots."

Susan knelt by the nearest raised bed. "Warm sunny days like today bring them out. This square gets the most early season sunshine. That's why the vegetables that get planted first go here – and always on March 17, St. Gertrude's Day – or if the ground's still frozen, on March 31, St. Detlaus' Day. This is the square that stands for the sun – the other three represent planets surrounding the center bed or 'heaven.'"

"And where the four paths meet it forms a cross," Rebecca said eagerly.

"That's why some folks call it the 'Cross Path,' like our Lord's cross. The bush planted in the center is called Crown of Thorns," Susan instructed. "Now, we need to get busy and break up these winter clods of dirt before another spring shower turns them to mud. Today is perfect. The sweet potato vines Mama has started in the kitchen window will go here. Then, if we have time, we can spread some of the tanbark from the tannery on the paths before the weeds get a head start on us."

"I'll take the trowel and turn over the dirt, and then you use the hand rake to break them up more. After that we can both pound the clumps with the back of our tools and work the soil with our hands until it's fine and light."

As they labored, Susan watched her younger sister out of the corner of her eye hoping that Rebecca would not notice her careful monitoring. Rebecca attacked the chore with the same enthusiasm that Susan recalled having on her first day of real gardening two years earlier.

"Better ease up a little, Rebecca. Your arms will be hurtin' you after supper tonight."

"But it feels good to be able to hit something as hard as I can – the way I'd like to hit that old Sean McBride when he starts in bullying Jacob. Sean knows Jacob's not allowed to fight. That's why he picks on him. I just pretend these old dirty lumps are Sean's bumpy old face and smash them. I hope the Lord isn't angry that it feels just grand. After all, Sean is none the worse for it, really."

Sarah smiled in agreement. "Well, we are taught to turn the other cheek and forgive with all our hearts, but it isn't easy. When Sean's mama starts pointing out every weed in the garden – or worse yet, makes some comment about how, 'David and Samuel just can't seem to find themselves wives,' I'd like to pound her to dust, too. Mama says just to ignore her remarks – that the McBrides are a little 'rough around the edges,' but that they have good hearts. I say what I've heard Papa say – 'the apple doesn't fall far from the tree.' I just know that I like to stay as far away from that family as I can."

Rebecca's arm paused in mid-swing as she considered Susan's statement. "I think you're absolutely right – especially if you call Papa the 'tree' and David the 'apple.' They get more like each other every day, but Papa's bad moods and orders are much easier to stand than David's. Sometimes I think David believes that he *is* Papa when it comes to bossing us around, and he's in a foul humor even more often than Papa."

Susan sighed. "That's true, and many days I've had more than my fill of David, but I guess we both need to remember that he's our brother. If God teaches us to try to love everyone, then surely that goes double for the members of our family."

Rebecca sat back on her heels. "That's not so hard with the others, you know – just David."

"I agree, but maybe he's so gruff and serious because he's the oldest son. If anything would happen to Papa, God forbid, then David would have to take over and help Mama as head of the family. That could weigh heavy on his mind and make him more cross than he might be if he didn't have that pressure," Susan said.

"Well, maybe. But if you ask me, I think he loves giving orders and being in charge," Rebecca said.

Susan didn't disagree.

"If you ask me *instead*," Susan echoed as she stabbed her trowel soundly into the soil, "I think we need to start working the dirt as much as we are working our mouths."

For the next few hours, small dust clouds followed their pounding and sifting as they worked their way up and down the rows.

As Susan worked, the images of her brother David's sour face stuck in the back of her mind like flour paste on a wooden spoon. It hung in the background of the afternoon's work and conversations as she and Rebecca transformed the soil into cushiony loam for planting. But, as the vision of his stern expression persisted, it began to change. From beneath the angry creases a softer sadness arose – a sadness that touched Susan and softened her as well.

Maybe David's so cross because he's sad, but he can't admit it because he thinks he might look weak. She sighed and paused her digging.

"Poor David," she said aloud.

"What?" asked Rebecca looking up at her sister, and not believing her ears.

"I said, 'poor David.'"

"David who?" Rebecca replied. "Surely not *our* David."

"Precisely our David. Think about it, maybe he's so mad because he's really sad."

Rebecca frowned. "Well, he certainly doesn't smile much – and I can't say that I've ever heard him laugh out loud."

"I have an idea," Susan said. "Why don't we help David to be happier?"

Rebecca blinked. "How?"

"I'm not sure how, but that's part of my idea. We need to figure out how to make him smile, and the first one who does, gets the other one's dessert for three days. What do you say?"

"You know how much I love Mama's desserts. I'm going to love having those double servings," Rebecca giggled.

-8-

DAY'S END

As the day's shadows lengthened, the gears of the Royer industrial farmstead wound down. With the grinding stones now still, Samuel locked the mill doors and gathered his abandoned roofing tools as Amos Fahnestock trudged home hauling his share of fresh flour in the wooden handcart behind him. The tannery workers, striped with grime and sweat, mounted the horses or mules that would carry them home and bring them back early the next morning. Daniel and David secured the heavy iron latch on the tannery door and wound their way up the path toward the log cabin. They rounded the ongoing construction of the new, two-story stone house quickly inspecting the progress made by the workers that day. The plow was leaning against the wall next to the mule's stall and the remaining fence rails were tucked around the corner of the barn door as John and Jacob scrubbed their arms up to their elbows with lye soap at the water trough pump.

Susan and Rebecca dangled their hands in the kitchen basin washing what they could of the garden's ash and dirt from the darkened half-moons of their fingernails. Cate was helping their mother spread the evening table as much as her slight stature would allow, while Polly swept the dirt floor smooth and even. Elizabeth had finished spinning the most recent cloud of wool from earlier sheep-shearing into yarn and was smoothing lard over baby Nan's red-rashed bottom as Catherine placed the last of the few leftovers from the noon meal – a kettle of corn mush and some slices of salt pork – on the table.

Five broad-rimmed black hats soon hung on wooden pegs by the door, and 11 familiar faces and a whimpering baby sat on both sides of the table. Growling stomachs would soon settle and weary muscles would rest to recoup for the demands of the next day.

The log walls of the Royers' modest cabin strained at the burgeoning family now settled in with the setting sun for the evening. Privacy was long since the victim of such close living quarters. Susan and Rebecca's teeth and gums still tingled with the bedtime ritual of scrubbing them with willow twig wands and baking soda. They lay face-to-face in their shared berth on the second floor loft, wide-eyed at the grumblings of their father that seeped through the walls as he instructed David and Samuel on the events of the day, particularly the encounter at the mill. Cate clutched her rag doll as she slept and her tiny butt cheeks found their familiar nightly niche in the small of Susan's back, the heat of her tiny body warming the chilly bedclothes.

As the lecture around the smoldering embers of the hearth intensified, Rebecca drew toward Susan and whispered so as not to alert older sisters Elizabeth and Polly in their small, but separate, beds on the far side of the loft. "I'm really thankful that God made me a girl, aren't you, Susan? Trouble seems to come at Papa from all sides and our brothers can only think their lives will be the same."

"The Lord most certainly knows what is best, but I think he gave girls sharp eyes and ears and the good sense to pay close attention to what troubles the menfolk so we can know best how to help them in our own way. Can you imagine how much worse it would be for Papa if Mama didn't provide him with good meals and an orderly house?" Susan said. She propped her head on her elbow for a view of any eavesdroppers before she continued.

The edge of Elizabeth's prayer book poked out from under her pillow and Susan suspected that Polly harbored the secret token from George Schmucker somewhere a bit safer. Their older sisters' breathing was steady and even – full of sleep. Pulling Rebecca's head to the pillow Susan confided, "That's why it's so important for Samuel to have a good wife –

a sweet girl like Sarah Provines. David is cantankerous enough to fend for himself, but Samuel needs and deserves the help of a strong woman."

"But what can we do, Susan? I'm sure David has set his cap for Sarah. He kept staring at her at last Sunday meeting, trying to catch her eye – and Samuel is no match for him most times."

"That's true, Rebecca, but I suspect that Sarah has her heart set on Samuel, not David. Last year at the corn shuckin' in Mathias's barn, she did everything but dance a jig to be near Samuel and avoid David."

Rebecca brightened. "You're right, Susan. You should have seen the way Sarah kept peeking around her broom today when Samuel and I were in town fetching those redware crocks for Mama. I could tell it pleased Samuel, though he didn't let her know directly. She even giggled when he smiled at her. When I asked him about it on the way home, he blushed beet red and pretended not to hear me."

"Maybe Samuel is just too modest to believe that Sarah prefers him to David. Or maybe he thinks David has more right to her because he's the oldest. Or maybe there is already some sort of agreement between Papa and Mr. Provines about the match that favors David? I'm sure no one would tell us. We're only the little sisters, you know? What is sure is that David won't be waiting much longer. He's nearly 23 and deaf if he doesn't know that folks like Mrs. McBride are noticing he's still a bachelor."

Rebecca grabbed hold of Susan's hand. "Susan, remember the story Omah Stoner told us about how she and Opah got together? Remember?"

Cate stirred in her sleep behind Susan. "Hush, Rebecca. You'll wake someone. What are you so excited about?"

"Omah's story. She said that the first time she saw Opah she thought he was the most handsome young man she'd ever seen, but he didn't seem to notice her. So the next time she knew she would see him, she put a bunch of dried forget-me-nots – she called them *fergess-mich-nerts* – under her shawl and Opah couldn't take his eyes off of her. Remember?"

"I think so. It's beginning to sound familiar. But, Samuel and Sarah have already noticed each other, so..."

"But what if the next time one of us goes to town with Samuel, we slip a tiny pouch of dried forget-me-nots in his pocket. It might push Sarah enough to say something to her papa about her feelings for Samuel, or it might set some other girls to noticing Samuel and make Sarah jealous enough to encourage Samuel more her way."

Susan drew up her lips and squinted. "I don't know, Rebecca. For a *kleine Schwester* you certainly come up with some pretty clever ideas. What if Samuel catches us putting it in his pocket? What would we say?"

"Well . . . ," she considered. "Maybe we could tell him it's a beanbag toy for Mrs. Provine's newest baby and ask him to keep it safe in his pocket for us. We could make another that looks just like it for the baby, but fill it with peony seeds like Nan's and hide it under our bonnets and make the switch at gifting time."

"Still seems too risky to me. If we do anything, let's keep it simple – just slip some in his pocket, if we can. Better to count on David's spilled salt at dinner to bring him bad luck, like losing ground with Sarah. The best thing might be to talk to Sarah the next time one of us goes to town and see if she's interested in bumping into Samuel in a less public place – some place we could just *happen* to make sure Samuel would be, if she *happened* to wander by. Maybe Samuel just needs the opportunity to speak his piece to her."

Rebecca scowled. "Could we still use the magic poultice somehow?"

Susan smiled. "We'll see. Now close your eyes and button your lips. Time to sleep."

The creaking of her brothers climbing the stairs to their beds in the loft under the opposite eave of the cabin was the last sound Susan heard until she was awakened by the early morning dancing of the rain on the rooftop only a few feet above her head.

-9-

SILVER LININGS

R ebecca rubbed her eyes. It was still dark, but the pounding of the rain on the wood shingle roof echoed in her ears. Baby Nan's mewing and the clank of iron pots being lowered over the fire joined the pelting chorus that called her from sleep to her morning chores.

"Oh fiddlesticks!' she groused. So much for her plan to escape to the woods this morning and look for yellow crocus and grape hyacinth that often poked their heads out through clumps of lingering snow. Slipping out from under the goosedown featherbed she shared with Susan and Cate, Rebecca quietly pulled her jumper over her head, tried to smooth her tight curls and pinned on her white cap. She tiptoed, barefoot, down the cool wood of the wear-polished stair treads.

She had hoped to pilfer a fistful of bread from last night's supper and sit outside under the porch to soak in the symphony of raindrops, but her mother was already in front of the low fire, rocking Nan and rubbing the teething baby's gums with a salve of crushed poppy seeds from the garden.

"You're the happy one this morning," said Catherine, mocking Rebecca's sullen frown. The girl couldn't hide her disappointment over yet another rainy day.

"Oh, Mama, why did it have to rain today? I'm so tired of being inside. I just want to be outside again. The daffodils down by the creek are beginning to bloom and I really wanted to bring some into the house to cheer us, but this awful rain just spoiled that."

"I know, *Liebling*, but this *awful* rain is good for the early planting. The Lord gives us what we need, not always what we want. Now, if you help me with breakfast, perhaps you and your sisters can dye some Easter eggs this afternoon. No time to *dopple*."

Rebecca's grimace melted as she spied the basket filled with newly hard-boiled eggs on the table.

So that's why Mama made us go to the chicken roost twice yesterday so as not to leave a single egg behind. Maybe this gloomy day won't be so depressing after all, she thought.

Easter marked the end of the season of Lent. For forty days leading up to the holy day they ate no cakes, cookies, pies or sweets of any kind as a reminder of Christ's suffering and death on the cross that was somberly recounted in Sunday services and in Daniel's nightly Bible readings. Easter represented Christ's triumph over the grave, but for Rebecca, it also meant the end of winter and the promise of spring's sweet warmth and fresh new life.

However foolish it might be, she always believed that winter would never leave until they decorated Easter eggs. When she and her sisters dipped the hard-boiled eggs into the bowls of color each year, Rebecca imagined the simmering beet juice that turned the delicate shells a rich pink and the dill seeds that created a deep gold were the same concoctions that coaxed the rosy petals of the redbud and the soft whites of the serviceberry trees into bloom.

She loved seeing the new dogwood and witch hazel buds pop out and plump into tender green leaves. Sometimes, even under pale April skies, the vibrant greens of the fields and trees almost hurt her eyes. After the blossoms littered the ground, could succulent strawberries and tart cherries be far behind? Though Rebecca's mouth watered at the thought, as the dank morning hours of late March seeped by, spring felt as far away as Christmas.

She scurried around the benches and table passing bowls of corn mush to her father and older brothers who came in shifts to the plank table. All were men of few words. The wet weather made their work harder. Only brother Samuel said *'Danke'* and winked at her when she placed the butter and the last of the brown bread in front of him. The men were barely fed and out at the mill or in the tanning yard before Catherine, Elizabeth and Polly hurried to bake fresh bread that had been rising on the sideboard since dawn.

The hearty noontime meal required six loaves and Catherine tried to stay ahead of her baking. Rebecca and Susan often helped with kneading the dough on the floured board, but their little fingers lacked the stamina to punch down the rising bread and repeat the process three or more times as the dough grew and grew until it was finally ready for the oven. *All that work*, thought Rebecca, *and then the slices just vanish the moment they meet the table!* She pushed the heel of her hand into the mound of warm dough on the table in front of her. *I would rather churn butter.*

The hustle and bustle of preparing and serving the noon meal, their main sustenance for the day, came and went without incident. Actually, the labor seemed lighter because of the promised fun that would follow the completed tasks. But as

Elizabeth and Polly placed the clean, dry clay tankards on the top shelf above the window – usually the final noon task – Catherine looked at her daughters' expectant faces. "Now, before the Easter eggs, we need to get a start on tomorrow's dinner." In the busy Royer household the end of one meal often signaled preparations for the next. As four pairs of shoulders drooped, she reminded them, "Our men need their strength, and John and Jacob will enjoy the *Hasenpfeffer* even more since they provided the rabbits from yesterday's hunting trip."

After what seemed an eternity, Catherine sprinkled dried herbs over the simmering stew that would be served at noon the next day and wiped her hands on her apron. She made a final survey of the cabin and after an extra teasing pause finally said, "Come girls, it's time."

Rebecca watched her mother pull ten colorful spatterware bowls from the corner cupboard. Decorated with brightly painted birds and flowers, the dishes had been manufactured in England specifically for the Pennsylvania Germans in the colonies. They were a gift from Catherine's parents when she first 'went to housekeeping' with Daniel. The cheerful designs and bold hues appealed to their love of nature and bright colors. Rebecca admired the bowls and felt a pang of pity for their Scotch-Irish neighbors who drank bitter tea from delicate, but drab, English porcelain.

The Royers preferred cider from sturdy tankards or an occasional mug of precious coffee, rather than the black tea their Scotch-Irish counterparts, particularly Mrs. McBride, made a great show of sipping from deep saucers of thin china. Rebecca recalled her mother's vivid description of having afternoon tea on McBride's front porch last April. The tea was brewed hot, poured into the cups, and then a tiny amount of the steaming liquid was transferred into the cup's wide and deep saucer to cool.

Rebecca harrumphed at the thought. *Mama said that she enjoyed the tea much more than the conversation.* Mrs. McBride had interrupted her unkind remarks about distant neighbors only long enough to slurp tea from the side of the saucer while she held the teacup in her right hand.

"I think it's just a lot of falderal ," Rebecca said. *Mama also told us that the china was very expensive and had spindly leaves and tiny, rust-colored flowers around the paper-thin rims – not nearly as cheery as ours.* She glanced at the Royer family's dinnerware awaiting its service at the next meal. The warm earth tones of the heavy platters and lively colors of the plates always made the vegetables and meats that accompanied the Royer's daily bread even more appetizing.

Mrs. McBride was so concerned about her precious cups that she never allowed her children to use them – even the ones with chipped rims. Their family normally ate their meals from dull, earthenware bowls and mugs with little or no decoration.

Not so at the Royers. *We get to see the beautiful colors of God's world in our dishes every day*, Rebecca thought with satisfaction. *If we happen to break a cup or bowl, Mama might scold, but we simply gather up the pieces, throw them down the privy and buy new ones that cost far less than the McBride's precious porcelain.*

Rebecca's thoughts of the sharp-tongued Mrs. McBride vanished as Catherine worked her rainbow magic brewing the colorful dyes. Each girl claimed a preferred color. Rebecca loved the shades of soft pink produced by a small quantity of beet juice, while Susan gave her brownish eggs a blue tint by soaking them in water boiled with red cabbage leaves. Elizabeth, of course, insisted on claiming the bowl steeped with steaming red onionskins.

"Red, to represent the blood of Christ shed for us," she offered primly.

Can't we just have some fun? implied Polly's silent gaze at the three younger girls at the end of the table. Rebecca struggled not to roll her eyes at Susan. Cate missed it all, lost in dunking her white orb in the green liquid that would soon transform her egg into a speckled work of art.

Polly realized almost at once that Mama would not appreciate her attitude and quickly prayed that her sisters would not laugh and give her away. Happily, they stifled their smiles and she was relieved that they did not break out into giggles and suffer Mama's stern reprimand.

Polly returned to dying her egg a shade of orange brewed from yellow onionskins. She turned it over and over again becoming unusually quiet. *It's the same color as George's auburn hair*, she thought.

"Hmm . . ." Rebecca considered as she noted Polly's dreamy eyes, but her thoughts were interrupted when Cate suddenly squealed. Her bowl had overturned and the green liquid made from boiled spinach leaves spread out across the table and dripped through the slits in the table planks onto the dirt floor.

"Now, now, Cate, don't cry," soothed Catherine moving to her side. "But let's leave the puddles outside, shall we? Besides, green is too calm a color for a sunny child like you. Let's boil up some chamomile tea and see if we can make a yellow egg or two." Cate's tears dried on her chubby cheeks as her mother used the edge of her apron to wipe the table.

As the number of painted eggs grew, Rebecca basked in the serenity of the moment, so unlike yesterday's turmoil and the adults' tense whispers last night. Whatever was troubling her elders was gone for now. She cherished these happy times with her mother and sisters. They were much more relaxed than when the men intruded with their worldly concerns. Here and now, her four sisters, her mother, and wide-eyed baby Nan were creating something lovely together – both the traditional Easter eggs and the peace. Her mother's often careworn face softened as they filled the cabin with laughter.

The decorated eggs would be the centerpiece on Easter morning, even if David pointed out the ones whose colors were inconsistent or accidentally splattered with color from other bowls. In Easters past, he had always blamed Rebecca for the eggs with cracked lines of color, even though it was little Cate in her youthful impatience who had fractured the shells. Rebecca would never blame the imperfect eggs on her more vulnerable sister, but David's cruelty irked her.

I'd like to see how well he could dip eggs with those doppish hands of his. He'd never have the patience to wait for the dyes to steep or gently roll the eggs in the bowl to cover them evenly. He might be a master miller, she thought bitterly, *but he shouldn't grind down our spirits like grain. He doesn't know anything about fun, or kindness either. If he's nasty again this year, I'll just hug Cate and tell David that the cracks look like delicate lace.*

All too soon, the fading light signaled that the time had come for the girls to pour out the colored liquid and wash and put away the bowls. Sad and strange how the hours spent with everyday chores like carrying gourds of water to the garden or sprinkling the plants with lime to discourage insects were endless, but hours passed having fun were over almost before they began. As soon as they rinsed the pretty dyes from the bowls, they would prepare the evening's light meal of bread and porridge. Only vigorous scrubbing with lye soap would clean their rainbow-stained hands, but as Rebecca playfully flicked water from the basin in Susan's direction, she noticed that the rain had stopped. The brightly-colored eggs now tucked safely on a high shelf had mane them forget about the grayness of the day.

The day would finally end as they bowed their heads at evening prayers and headed off to bed. *This has been a good day after all*, she mused. She glanced at the stars beginning to blink in the clearing sky. *Thank you, God for the awful rain.* Then her smile stretched more as the warm air of the cabin reminded her, *and tomorrow . . . we'll be having rabbit stew!*

-10-

SUSAN'S TRIP TO TOWN

David and Samuel bounced the family's sturdy work wagon over the rough and rocky road to town. It was Susan's turn to go to Waynesburg with her older brothers, and she was grateful for the pile of hay Samuel had tossed into the wagon bed. The dry chaff stirred by the jostling sprinkled into her eyes and crept up her nose, but it also cushioned the bumps and saved her many bruises and scrapes. She paid little heed to her brothers' conversation because her mind was bursting at the seams as she rehearsed the conversation she hoped to have with Sarah Provines. A prodigious ridge of shale on the dirt highway threw the wagon a formidable jolt. David's wide-brimmed hat hopped to a precarious slant on his thick, dark hair. He grunted as he snatched it back and shoved it squarely into its proper position.

Samuel called to the back of the wagon. "Are you still with us, Susan? That was quite a bump."

"Still here," she called out.

"I suppose this is what Papa meant about needing to improve the roads," Samuel told David who scrambled to regain a firm rein on the team of horses hauling them up the lane.

"Of course it is," David said. "Those clans of Lehmans and such seem to think they're too good . . ." he snapped the whip beside the struggling team, " . . . too much better than us to pay their due. It took all *Vater* had to keep from hitting Mr. Lehman at the mill the other day."

"It seems that others don't always see things the way we do. Guess that's their right and privilege," Samuel said.

David glared at him. "And they'll make it their 'right and privilege' to use the roads we improve just the same."

Samuel shrugged, knowing it was useless to disagree with David.

"When are you going to toughen up, Samuel? Letting people walk all over you is a disgrace." He cracked the whip just above the horses' ears again and Samuel cringed feeling sorry for the beasts that were suffering because of the argument that had nothing to do with them.

"Like our nosy neighbor." David tipped his head to the left in the direction of the McBride's small cabin on the acreage adjoining the Royer property. "What business is it of hers if you and I aren't married yet? Doesn't she have enough to do keeping track of her own brood?"

"I see your point," said Samuel, "but it is true that many others our ages and younger have started their own families by now. Don't you ever think about that, David?"

"Of course, I do, but from what I've seen, the pickings are pretty slim. Surely, very few of the available girls around here can measure up to Mama. The only one I can recall who even comes close is Sarah Provines." Samuel tightened at the mention of the name, but David continued on, unaware of his brother's reaction. "She's pleasant, not hard to look at, and her father's business is booming. That's a real added bonus. No use inheriting debt along with a wife, if you can help it."

Samuel had no reply, but resented the implication that Sarah Provines needed any bonus other than her own sweet self to offer a prospective husband.

Susan hunched in the straw mound behind them knowing they had pretty much forgotten she was there. David's voice made her quiver.

Surely Sarah Provines will prefer Samuel's sweetness, she thought. *I just have to get her alone and hope she'll agree to meet Samuel by accident at next Sunday meeting.*

She squeezed the rag doll wrapped in her apron – the gift she would tell Samuel she had to deliver to Mrs. Provines for the family's newest baby. Rebecca's scheme of forget-me-nots had been put off until a later time. It was best to keep their current plot as simple as possible.

Waynesburg was bustling with activity, as usual, on a pleasant summer day. David backed the wagon to the rear door of George Besore's general store. The shipment of sand and iron parts for the on-going construction of their new home would be a heavy load for her brothers to haul home. She studied the large pile of supplies that awaited them.

Sehr gut, she thought. *I should have plenty of time to talk to Sarah.*

She tucked the new rag doll into the crook of her arm and tapped Samuel's shoulder. "May I take this gift to Mrs. Provines for her new baby now?"

Samuel crouched down to her height. He eyed the doll. "Looks like you did a fine job with your gift," he said. "Just make sure you're not too long. We need to leave as soon as the wagon is loaded. It will be a long, hard trip for the horses."

Susan smiled. "I will, Samuel. I promise."

With David out of earshot, Samuel stood and added casually without looking at her, "By the way, if you see Sarah, kindly remember to give her my best."

"Oh, I will," she said. *I most surely will*, she thought as she sped away.

The wooden barrels that Ezra Provines crafted at his cooperage were the most reliable to be had in the entire county.

His business was doing very well and more than adequately supported his ever-growing family. Sarah was his eldest and, just as the older girls in Susan's family, had her hands full helping her mother with the younger children and other household chores. Their home was just a few blocks past the workshop and not far from the store where Susan had left her brothers at their labors.

As she turned the corner toward her destination, Susan saw she was in luck. A gust of breeze lifted the damp work shirt that hung from the clothesline strung between two trees in the Provines's side yard and revealed that the two legs that were visible below the string of drying clothes and diapers belonged to Sarah. No one else was in sight.

Susan threw her hand in the air and called out – loud enough to alert Sarah but no one else – "Hello, Sarah."

Sarah was bent over the straw basket beside her choosing the next item to hang. Hearing her name, she paused and looked up at Susan's approach.

"Hello?" she answered as she dropped the wet apron in her hand and stood up to push aside the dangling shirt to see who had called. She smiled when she discovered the source. "Oh, Susan," she called. "What a nice surprise. It's good to see you. Would you like to come . . .?"

Susan snapped her finger up to her lips. "Shhh." She grasped the rag doll under her arm and beckoned for Sarah to come over.

Sarah looked puzzled.

"Come here," Susan said in a loud whisper.

Sensing the need for secrecy, Sarah checked behind her for any witnesses. Seeing none, she pushed the few remaining items down in the basket so a stray wind wouldn't carry them into the dusty yard and followed Susan to the far end of the walkway that lead to the Provines's front porch. It afforded a clear vantage point to see anyone who might approach close enough to hear.

"What is it, Susan?" said Sarah looking puzzled.

"I brought this doll for your new baby sister." She extended the gift to Sarah.

"How thoughtful," said Sarah holding it at arm's length to admire it properly. It's adorable. Did you make it yourself? Leah will love it."

"Yes," Susan said smiling. "It's just like the one my sister Elizabeth made for my baby sister, Nan. But, this isn't the only reason I'm here. I want to ask you something."

"I'm listening," said Sarah cradling the doll tenderly in her arm.

Susan motioned her to come closer. Sarah bent down becoming a willing player in the younger girl's endearing drama.

"Are you coming to Sunday meeting at the Lesher's this week?" Susan said behind her hand.

"I plan to. Just about everyone who is able goes to Sunday meetings."

"That's good," Susan said. "I mean . . ." she hesitated. Then she blurted, "Do you get poison ivy itch?"

"Actually, I got a horrible, itchy rash last fall when I picked some wild flowers in the field next to a patch of ivy," answered Sarah, wondering where the conversation was going.

"Really!" Susan had to stop herself from jumping for joy. "I mean, really," she repeated with less enthusiasm. "Well, Mama says that the best thing to stop the itch is to rub the leaves of Deadly Nightshade on the rash, but they are really hard to find. Most folks have gotten rid of them because it sickens the cows if they eat them. Nightshade plants are easier to spot in late summer because they get little bright red berries and climb on other plants."

"I've heard that, too," said Sarah.

Susan continued almost breathless, "I heard that a stubborn patch of Deadly Nightshade is growing down by the creek near the big sycamore tree at the Lesher's house. Actually, Samuel knows exactly where it is. He gets terrible ivy itch, too. I think if you go down to that sycamore after the service at this Sunday's meeting, I'm sure he would be happy to show you."

Sarah smiled to herself, but managed to maintain a serious expression. "I just might be able to do that. Thank you for letting me know."

"Oh, you're welcome," Susan said. "See you Sunday, then?"

Sarah nodded. "And I'll make sure to show Mama the pretty gift you made for Leah."

"What?" Susan stammered and then quickly remembered her ploy for the visit. " . . . I mean, yes, please do show her the rag doll. Give her my family's best regards and God's love."

"I certainly will – and I will certainly see you at Sunday meeting."

Their eyes caught in an acknowledgement of mutual confidence. Susan gathered up her skirt. "Well . . . I've got to go. David and Samuel will be waiting for me at the general store." She whirled around and dashed away, then pulled up short and looked back at Sarah who was watching her hasty departure. "Oh, I nearly forgot. Samuel asked me to say 'Hello' to you."

"How sweet. Please give him my fondest regards, too," Sarah said.

"I will, Sarah," she agreed as she resumed her retreat.

I certainly will, she thought to herself. *Wait 'til I tell Rebecca. She won't believe our luck any more than I do!*

Slowing to a less suspicious stride as she turned the corner, she noticed Samuel leaning against the heavily laden wagon with his arms crossed watching some children play in the street nearby.

Her 'fondest regards,' Susan recalled Sarah's words as she looked at her brother. *'Fondest regards.'* Her heart skipped. Then she noticed David following Mr. Besore into the store to pay. It was nearly time to leave; she had completed her mission just in time.

It can't be just luck, she thought as she glanced up at the white clouds dotting the sky. *It surely must be God's will that Samuel and Sarah be together.* She closed her eyes. *Please, dear Lord.*

In an open stretch of ground near the rear entrance to the general store, five or six youngsters stirred up the dust scurrying about in a small, but intense game of rounders. One of the boys had just hit the fabric-stuffed leather ball with a large flat stick and was attempting to run around a 30-foot circle designated by five sticks before someone retrieved the ball and hit him with it. The shortest member of the group scooped up the rolling ball and flung it at the runner.

"Stop running, Levi. You're out!" yelled the thrower.

"You missed me by a mile," Levi retaliated.

As the two boys argued looking to their teammates for support, the runaway ball bounced into the lap of a young girl who sat placidly on a small quilt in a patch of grass shaded by the Remmel family's wagon parked close to the Royer's. She had been passively watching the other children play. Startled, she stared at the ball with her deep-set, slanted eyes and smiled broadly. Her pudgy fingers grasped awkwardly for the ball to throw it back. Before she could coordinate her movements to complete the toss, one of the boys snatched the ball away without acknowledging her at all. Her shoulders sagged and she began fumbling with the edge of the quilt as she cocked her head to the side and stared into space.

Samuel, watching the scene unfold, recognized Nellie, her small drooping mouth and broad nose shadowed by the brim of her white bonnet. Every Sunday meeting, she sat at her mother's side swinging her legs and turning her tattered blanket over and over. At times during the long service, Mrs. Remmel had to shush Nellie's inarticulate conversations with her blanket, her only companion, as she was unable to play with the other children. Rarely was she away from her home, except to attend church with her family. Today she was with her father who stood a few steps behind her discussing business with Mr. Michael Corkery, one of the most important men in town.

Samuel pushed away from the wagon and picked a few wild buttercups from the patch he had noticed near the edge of the grass plot. Then he knelt beside Nellie. She continued to gaze up and away from him, but he murmured, "These flowers are my favorite color, Nellie – yellow."

Her head dropped slightly in his direction. "Could you take care of them for me? I have a long, hot ride home, and they look lovely with your pretty dress." He saw her smile to the air.

Mr. Remmel stopped in mid-business when he noticed someone with Nellie, but made no move to interfere when he recognized Samuel. At the same time, Mr. Provines rounded the corner rolling a large wooden barrel that Daniel Royer had ordered the previous week. He, too, stopped short when he saw Samuel at Nellie's side.

Samuel tenderly took Nellie's hand from her lap and opened it. When he laid the buttercups in her palm, she closed her fingers and turned to him. Her face scrunched into a broad grin and she bounced up and down with delight. Samuel chuckled, "Just look at that beautiful smile. You must like yellow, too, Nellie."

"Samuel! Stop your folly and load that barrel on the wagon," shouted David as he exited the back door of the store.

Mr. Remmel and Mr. Provines shot incensed looks at David, who remained oblivious. Samuel winced inwardly, but did not hurry his exchange with Nellie, though David's abrupt call had made her jump. He leaned in and kissed the top of her bonnet.

"Thank you so much for taking care of my flowers. I have to go now." Her smile faded. Samuel continued, "That silly brother of mine must think your name is 'Folly.' God bless you, Nellie."

As Samuel rose, he nodded to Mr. Remmel who returned the gesture. By that time, Mr. Provines had nearly reached the Royer's wagon with his delivery. Samuel met him at the rear of wagon and they bent down in tandem, grabbed the lower edges of the barrel and shoved it into the last open corner of the wagon.

Mr. Provines extended his hand to Samuel who returned a firm handshake. "Tell your father it is a pleasure doing business, and I thank you for your help, young man."

"I will tell him, Sir, and you're quite welcome."

"Susan!" David chided his sister standing a few yards down the street. He was seated behind the team clutching the reins anxious to depart. "Stop your daydreaming and find a place in the back."

"Coming, David," she called running toward the wagon.

Samuel snagged her under her arms and landed her lightly on top of a large sandbag among the pile of provisions.

"Into the wagon," said David.

Samuel then heaved himself up beside David who shook his head. "What foolishness. You're hopeless, Samuel."

"Oh, I have more hope than you know, Brother," said Samuel calmly, inviting no confrontation.

Susan secured a firm hold on the edges of the sandbag. *Even more hope than you know yourself, Samuel*, she thought. She could hardly wait to give him Sarah's message, but knew it was best to deliver it when they were alone. Better not to alert David.

Mr. Provines watched the Royer's wagon leave a powdery track as it disappeared down Main Street.

Calloused hands and a compassionate heart – a good man that Samuel Royer, he thought. *A very good man.*

-11-

Summer Comes to Call

The extended daylight of summer delighted the Royer children in spite of the extra hours of work on their flourishing farmstead. The heat of this particular day had percolated the creek water into an oppressively humid steam bath. Susan and Rebecca completed the hoeing and the more pleasant watering of the parched four-square garden with dipper gourds and clay watering bells that were fed from the large oaken bucket of cool stream water. As the temperature rose, they herded the farm ducks inside the garden fence to gobble up the hateful insects that were so destructive to the plants. The girls had worked too hard to sacrifice their bounty of thriving squash, potatoes, cabbages, beans and such to the pests.

The eggplants were beginning to blush purple under their protective burlap tents and the potato and cabbage leaves were powdered with white lime dust from the family's small kiln to discourage the disgusting slugs. As Rebecca plopped one of the slimy, swollen marauders into her leather bucket to drown, she said to Susan, "I know that the Lord made all creatures, but what was he thinking when he made these?" She scowled at another squirming intruder pinched between her fingers.

"I know what you mean," Susan said. "Mosquitoes, too." She rubbed the inside of her wrist against her rough work apron to ease the itchy bumps of her most recent rash of annoying bites. "But, like Mama says, 'the ways of the Lord are mysterious – not for us to understand or question.'" She scratched again. "Still, I can't help but think the world could do with a few less creatures."

Rebecca tossed another disgusting slug into her bucket. "Too bad the *Butzemann* and *Butzefrau* don't frighten the slugs like they do most of the crows."

She looked at Mr. and Mrs. Scarecrow stationed at opposite ends of the garden. Their imposing height and worn garments flapping in the breeze discouraged many of the marauding birds.

"Maybe we should have made them a little less handsome." Susan smiled.

A random breeze combed the leaves on the heavily-foliaged oak trees and carried the scent of the nearby patch of peppermint to the girls who lifted their heads to catch the cooling current in the brims of their sunbonnets. Susan glanced at the fragrant green plantings near the garden gate and found Polly harvesting a small bouquet of stalks. "Mama needs some more mint to add to the herb tea to fight this heat. It must be just terrible in the tannery today." Polly explained before she dashed back to the cabin where she was helping Catherine with noon meal preparations.

"I bet she puts an extra sprig in George Schmucker's mug," said Rebecca.

Susan nodded, "And she's been chewing sweet cicely like it's Mama's horehound candy, too, to freshen her breath, I think."

They shared a giggle as they continued down the rows.

Little Cate knelt beside baby Nan on a well-worn woolen blanket spread on the floor in a corner of the cabin. She shook a rattle of strung peony seeds just out of her baby sister's reach. Everyone had a job. Cate's was to mind Nan to free Mama for her multitude of other tasks. Nan's was to coo peacefully as Elizabeth and Polly served as additional kitchen crew.

Catherine fluffed the vase of Toad Balsam placed in the cabin window as a deterrent to the mosquitoes. "Take that you nasty bugs." She scraped her work-worn fingernails over the red welts that peppered the back of her neck.

As she studied the recent framing of their new home through the window, she sighed. "They can't finish that lovely house too soon for me." The large four-bedroom structure would be much grander than their humble cabin, but the design adhered to the modest rooflines, windows and other subdued features preferred by those of their faith. The sin of pride was never far from their minds, but Catherine was, indeed, thankful that their family had been so amply blessed.

The same small breeze that had swept through the four-square garden caught the Toad Balsam and tickled her chin. "I guess that next summer we'll need a lot more vases of this to chase all the pesky biters from so many new rooms." She closed her eyes imagining the day she would open their new front door and inhale the scent of blessed space – room to stretch and grow.

As she drew in a deep breath, Polly arrived with the mint and broke her mother's fleeting daydream. "Here, Mama."

"*Gut*, swish it with some water and put it in the tea crock." Catherine carried the rye basket of warm bread to the table and took a final inventory for the impending feast. The freshly gathered *Dresdner alleriei*, a mixture of carrots and peas, surely brightened the array. As Elizabeth laid the last of the wooden spoons by the plates, Catherine said, "Time to ring the bell, Polly."

Across the newly scythed ten-acre field of hay, the clang of the dinner bell from the front porch of the cabin stopped Jacob and John's joint effort to secure one of the many bales that had challenged them since dawn. The recent spell of dry weather was the best time to harvest with less chance that the bundles would rot and mildew from rain in the months to come. The hearty meal would fuel them for the long afternoon of hauling the bales to the shelter of the barn. They brushed the golden twigs from their clothes and headed toward the cabin.

John enjoyed a surge of self-confidence as he realized he had to duck his head as he stepped onto the front porch to avoid the asparagus switches that hung from the eaves. Last summer they had barely tousled the light-brown hair on the top of his head. The bundles dangled from barn and cabin rafters to ward off troublesome summer flies.

Susan and Rebecca followed closely behind. Their route from the garden took them past the outdoor privy. They gave it a wide berth and tried not to breathe as they passed. Thankfully, the bright-orange, knee-high daylilies they had planted around the perimeter of the outhouse last fall had significantly lessened the odor. No wonder the flowers also had another name, craproot. The fragrant honeysuckle vine clinging to the rough wooden sides of the small structure also helped when it was in bloom.

Samuel made his way down from the gristmill. A paste of flour and sweat plastered every crevice of his arms and face. As he passed one of the adjacent cherry trees, he cradled his hand under a low hanging bough and lifted it. The weight confirmed what the fruit's color and aroma had suggested. His younger siblings would need to be picking them soon. In fact, he felt some of the tiny, tart fruit that had already dropped to the ground crush under his shoes.

He plucked a small cluster and popped the dark red cherries into his mouth. As he spit out the pits, he snatched two more large handfuls to share with the others at the table. The pungent juices dripped down his chin and made him think of Mama's cherry pies baked in flakey, buttery crust. He spat two more pits onto the ground before following his younger sisters through the door. He piled his colorful offering on the long table – a fistful at each end.

Susan and Rebecca turned to see what Samuel was doing. He thought that their looks were meant to thank him, but instead, their eyes popped a bit and they looked at each other and covered their mouths to muffle their laugher. Before he could question their reaction, they scurried to the kitchen pump to complete the compulsory wash up before eating. Mama was very strict about this house rule – even Papa complied.

David then marched in the door from the tannery, his clothes mottled dark and wet with perspiration. He started to hang his hat by the door, but balked and stared at Samuel. He frowned, moved closer and roughly swiped Samuel's chin with his filthy hand.

"What's this silly pink slime on your chin?"

Samuel touched his face in confusion and then realized the cherry juice had tinted the flour coating his face a blushing pink. Now he understood his sisters' amusement.

"Oh, it's only . . . ," he started to explain.

David cut him off. "Wash off that girlish mess."

The girls sobered up immediately. Catherine sensed the tension in the air and turned toward David and Samuel who were staring hard at each other.

"What's the matter?" she asked.

"Nothing, Mama," Samuel answered, finally breaking eye contact with David and moving toward the pump.

David said nothing, though he knew his mother was waiting for his confirmation. The only movement in the room was Samuel's washing and Nan's wiggling in Elizabeth's arms.

Daniel's footsteps on the porch abruptly ended the standoff as everyone hastily resumed their normal activities. All understood instinctively that Papa's peace of mind always took precedence. "Looks like the carpenters have almost finished framing the new house," he said as he entered. "Won't be long before the walls are . . ." The tension in the air made him stop mid-sentence.

The uncommon focus that everyone was giving their actions robbed Daniel of his usually attentive audience. Though this puzzled him, he could identify no obvious conflict to address, so he moved to the space by the pump vacated by Samuel and proceeded to clean up.

David remained rooted to his spot. Elizabeth laid Nan in her cradle and shimmied by David close enough to whisper, "Pray, be calm, Brother," before she took her seat. David moved slowly to the pump, but barely moistened his hands at first. Then he scrubbed fiercely as the family waited for his presence at the table so Daniel could offer the blessing. The others stared holes into their plates as David moved to his place behind the bench at his father's right hand.

Daniel looked down the length of the table at Catherine who nodded ever so slightly. Then he folded his hands and bowed his head. The rest at the table followed suit and he began, "Father, bless this food and grant that peace be with us this day. Make us ever mindful of thy bountiful goodness which . . ."

-12-

Sunday Meeting

Most of the remaining corn crop was ready to yield all it could for the year. The daylight hours had been getting shorter for well over a month. The four-square garden was in various stages of harvest and some beds were fallow waiting for the fall planting of turnips and parsnips. It wouldn't be long before the stands of deciduous trees – the oaks and maples – would take on their bright autumn scarlet, persimmon, and ochre. Although some afternoons could slip into sweltering summer heat, the mornings and evenings were blessedly cooler.

This crisp September Sunday morning had dawned wearing robin's egg blue skies and a shawl of cozy sunshine. A brief shower the night before had tamed the dust clouds that would have been trailing behind the Royer's wagons as they made their way some four miles across rough country roads to the Lesher's home for Sunday meeting. The air smelled clean and crisp and the sky was a hypnotizing backdrop to the details of the countryside that stood out with crystal clarity. The flax bundles that had stood in the fields just a month earlier had been retted in the stream and dried enough to begin the laborious scutching and heckling to produce the silken strands that would  be spun into linen thread. Soon the golden corn shocks would take their place in adjacent fields and be transformed into meal and syrup and even whiskey for sale or trade. But, today was not for such labor – Sunday was for worship and fellowship.

The men's wagon led the way on the rutted trail with Daniel at the reins. Samuel sat in the back having ceded his usual seat beside Papa to Jacob so that his 12-year-old brother could get more experience handling the team of horses he would be expected to drive someday.

Susan and her sisters shared the back of the second wagon driven by David with Catherine seated beside him holding Nan. Polly had charge of the hog maw, her mother's specialty of pig's stomach stuffed with potatoes, sausage and herbs, as their contribution to the shared noon meal, and Elizabeth steadied the carefully packed basket of dishes for the family. Nearly 80 brethren would break bread together after 'church.'

As always, Rebecca and Susan were wedged together just behind the driver's bench. Today they were bursting with anticipation – not for the three or four lengthy sermons and hours of echoing slow-paced hymns led by the elder – not for enduring the hard benches that had been delivered the day before to the Lesher's barn for their hosting day – not even for the delicious meal that would be served outside under the trees after the service. This Sunday meeting promised to be special. The girls had reviewed the details of their objective for the day before they climbed into the wagon; they didn't want anyone else to overhear. It was all they could do to maintain the semblance of this being any other Sunday morning. If the service dragged on and the heat rising from the barn floor and the droning voices made Rebecca's eyelids droop, a well-disguised poke from Susan's elbow would remind her of their secret mission.

All had gone well thus far. Rebecca had even managed to slip a tiny handful of *fergess-mich-nerts* into Samuel's back pocket when she startled him with an unsolicited hug at breakfast. Only yesterday he had developed a rash from picking some wild daisies that Susan had requested for the table the week before knowing they were very close to a small patch of poison ivy. She felt a tinge of regret that he would have to endure the awful itch, but her purpose, she hoped, would out-weigh his discomfort. Perhaps some Deadly Nightshade would even magically appear under the tree down by the creek at the Lesher's where she had suggested he check after Sunday meeting. If not, she had reserved enough of the succulent thick leaves of the Hens and Chicks from the four-square garden to make a soothing salve.

She rested her chin under the cushion of her folded hands on the bouncing, wooden edge of the wagon. As she searched the sky for any fleeting white clouds, she thought, *Surely the Lord is showing He is with us by granting us such a perfect day.* She had been praying all week for just such Sunday weather. *But as Mama says, 'the Lord chooses the requests He will answer.'*

"Tuck those curls up in your bonnet, Sarah," scolded Mrs. Provines as she and her daughters made their way to the women's side entrance of the Lesher's barn. She stepped aside and stopped Sarah with her. "Here, hold the baby while I fix your hair properly. Don't want tongues wagging about you during meeting, now do you?"

"No, Mama," she answered taking her newest sister Leah in her arms. She stared at the rag doll Susan Royer had delivered earlier wrapped in the baby's blanket and thought about Samuel. *Maybe I can manage to pull out just one little curl at the back of my neck when Mama's not looking*, she connived silently. *If Samuel sits on the men's side behind me, maybe he'll notice. Dear Lord, I know that vanity is a sin, but if it's to please a godly man like Samuel, is it so terrible? After all, the Lord gave me the curls, didn't He?'*

Sarah winced as her mother firmly hid the last tendril under her daughter's white cap. "I don't know where your mind has been lately, Sarah," she said. She laid a hand on Sarah's shoulder, and then reached for Leah. "You're usually my responsible *Leibchen*. Did you coat your ankles well with the itch salve this morning?"

"Yes, Mama."

"I thought you learned your lesson last year when you took that same shortcut around the back of the garden – right through the same patch of poison ivy that got you before. Mind now, no scratching during the service."

"Yes, Mama," she agreed. She regretted sacrificing a bit of her reputation for reliability with her mother, but the deliberate case of poison peppering her ankles would make her planned visit to the creek after the service more believable. Samuel, if he showed up as Susan had hinted, mustn't see her as over anxious.

The Sunday crowd was swelling to its typical size as worship time drew closer. A bevy of women stood at the side entrance. A formidable group of hardy, bearded men and boys had gathered at the front double door embracing and welcoming each other with the traditional kiss of brotherhood. The usual familiar topics bounced between them. The more elder discussed crops, weather and livestock, along with a few more intense discussions about differing views within the congregation. The younger, unmarried *men* – generally older teens to younger 20's – talked of less serious issues and put their heads together in more hushed tones about which young ladies were 'growing up quite well.'

David drifted toward his more senior brethren, uncomfortable with such frivolous talk. He would choose a wife soon enough without anyone else's input, regardless of the opinions of shrews and gossips.

Samuel preferred to stay close to his peers and kept a sharp ear for the mention of Sarah Provines' name. He smiled as worship time approached and he still hadn't heard any other young man speak of her. Surely they were blind to her beauty, but that was their problem - definitely not his. Perhaps for now David might be his only competition.

The chorus of busy voices hushed as the congregation took their places on the narrow, rough wooden benches. A sense of order and the communion of common fellowship filled the barn. The seats were made of sturdy oak and had withstood multiple handlings as they were transported from one home to another in succession as the Sunday meeting changed hosts among the brethren. They were arranged in two sections on either side of a center aisle.

Men sat on the right facing the front and women on the left. All wore The Garb, dark trousers with suspenders and shirts with thin band collars or modest dresses with shawls and plain white caps with chin ties. As soon as they married, men grew full beards, but shaved their mustaches. Younger girls could wear their long hair in braids during the week, but at Sunday meeting they pulled their tresses into severe buns beneath their white caps, like their older sisters and mothers. All were equal before God's eyes and the uniformity of dress helped the brethren combat the sin of pride.

There was no traditional church altar, but every Sunday the impressive Long Table that traveled with the benches stood prominently up front. Behind it sat the three elders who were designated that day to deliver the scripture message and various interpretive scripts – some original, some copied from old texts of the church.

Maneuvering herself into a lead position, Sarah led the Provines women to one of the forward-most rows, a particularly advantageous spot in her opinion. As she arranged her skirts for the lengthy service, she managed to *accidentally* bump Leah's doll to the barn floor. Leaning over to retrieve it, she stole a glance behind her trying to discover where Samuel was seated.

From among the sea of beards and suspenders, she spied his unruly shock of golden-brown hair as he settled his broad-brimmed hat in his lap. He had a nearly perfect vantage point for the curl that she had managed to release again at the nape of her neck.

When Elder Strickler rose from his chair and stood behind the stark, but heavily polished Long Table, all eyes were on him. He clasped his hands in front of him and bowed his head without a word. Everyone bowed their heads except little Nellie Remmel who studied the heavy barn rafters and swung her legs in a steady cadence that she would maintain for the hours to come.

Prayer was a private matter between each individual and God. The Lesher's barn was transformed by a charged silence. A building that usually sheltered farm animals became a place of worship, full of a spirit that transcended sound and connected earth with the mysteries of the Kingdom in each person's thanks and petitions to his Almighty. After a goodly time, Elder Jones pronounced a solemn Amen and began his oration.

Although musical instruments were permitted in Lutheran and Moravian services, they were absent from German Baptist worship. Rebecca had once heard her father remark that organs and brass horns did not belong at Sunday meeting. 'A devilish distraction,' she remembered him saying. In German

Baptist services the presiding elder would intone, or *line*, hymns one phrase at a time that the congregation would then repeat as they followed along the verses printed in their palm-sized *Gesangbuch*.

Part of most families' nightly rituals throughout the week was instructing the children in the more commonly used Biblical passages or parables. Often they also reviewed and reinforced the belief statements of their German Baptist faith that permeated every aspect of their lives. Sunday meeting was a time for holy worship, not instruction.

As Samuel raised his head at Elder Strickler's "Amen," he let his gaze wander across the center aisle. Row upon row of gauzy, white-capped heads at staggered heights, from the upper tier of adults to the diminutive peaks of the youngest girls, blurred his focus. Then he spied it – the light-chestnut silken wisp resting on Sarah Provines' neck. It would repeatedly challenge his devotions until the final Amen almost three hours later.

"Tell Mama that I'll be right back to help with the meal," Sarah told her ten-year-old sister, Magdelena. "I've got to go down to the creek to see if I can find some plants to help this awful poison itch." She lowered her sock enough to show her sister the rosy rash as proof.

Without waiting for a response, Sarah headed for the large sycamore on the creek bank some 200 yards from where the men were laying planks across sawhorses to assemble the large makeshift picnic tables. Sarah had not risked asking her mother's permission to leave fearing she might not agree. She crossed her fingers as she scanned the greener grasses under the shade of the spreading old tree. The women who had been seated around her for the worship service had moved slower than molasses in January in exiting the barn. *He may have come and gone already*, she fretted to herself resisting the urge to break into an over-anxious run.

Samuel stood by the quiet creek studying the fresh green vine in his hand. The leaves were the right shape —one large center lobe and two smaller wing-like lobes at the base, but no red berries.

"I hope Susan knows what she was talking about," he muttered rubbing the irritating rash on his forearm. He squatted by the stream and continued his search, scouting the bank closer to the edge of the woods for encouraging specks of red. A frog, startled by his approach leapt into the water. The noon sun shimmered along the ripples of the widening rings on the disrupted calm surface. The shiny circles caught Samuel's eye and transformed them into a familiar silken curl. He paused and smiled. Then a shadow popped up from the border of shade cast along the side of the bank by the ancient sycamore. He turned his head to investigate and caught his breath when he saw Sarah standing behind him.

"Hello, Sarah." Samuel arose, still holding the vine in his hand.

"Hello, Samuel," she said trying to act surprised to see him.

He showed the plant to Sarah. "I was just here looking for some Deadly Nightshade to ease the itch of the poison ivy. I've heard that it's even better than the salve my mother makes from the Hens and Chicks plants from the garden."

"That's why I'm here, too," she said. "I wandered through a patch of that nasty ivy along the fence row at home last week." She bent over and vigorously rubbed her ankle.

"And this summer heat makes the itch even worse, doesn't it?" Samuel added attacking the rash on his forearm.

"Your sister, Susan, told me that I might find the Deadly Nightshade here. "In fact," she said, "she said that if you were here, you might be able to help me find it."

"Oh," he replied trying to disguise his immediate suspicions about his sister and this *chance* meeting with Sarah. "I think . . . I mean, I haven't had much luck yet. The leaves look something like this." He handed her the bit of vine. "But it should have small red berries this time of year."

As she took the offering from him, their hands touched. They both hesitated and instinctively smiled. Their cheeks flushed as they moved a modest step away from each other.

"W . . .Well," Sarah stammered, "four eyes should be better than two. Don't you think?"

"Absolutely," Samuel said. "I was thinking it might be a bit further on down the creek bank on the right."

"Let's have a look."

As they neared the stream, Samuel offered her his hand. "Watch your step, Sarah. It's a little slippery here."

Sarah felt perfectly grounded, but didn't hesitate to accept his offer. "Oh, look," she said pointing with her other hand. "I think I see something red right over there."

As she stepped forward leading Samuel toward the plant, her foot landed on a moss-covered rock hidden beneath the long grass and she tumbled backwards. Samuel instinctively dove to break her fall. Catching her shoulders, he was thrown off balance and the both ended in a heap on the soft bank.

"Sarah!" Are you hurt?" Samuel righted himself and pulled her to his chest, away from the stream.

Sarah threw her arms around Samuel's neck to steady herself. In an instant they were nose to nose. They gazed at each other.

"I'm fine, Samuel" she whispered.

"You are, indeed," he said as he lowered his lips to hers. She didn't resist and gently returned the brief kiss. They paused for a second look, and then backed away from each other until they were seated side-by-side staring at the water and holding hands. They would linger there as long as they dare without raising suspicions. Such meetings would need the approval of their families to be proper.

"Where is that sister of yours? Didn't she tell you she would be here to help *schnell*?" Mrs. Provines and Magdelena laid out the last of the family table as baby Leah starting fussing for her overdue nursing.

"Here she comes now, Mama. Up from the creek, like I told you." Then Magdelena's eyes widened. She skirted closer to her mother and whispered. " . . . and Samuel Royer's with her . . . and they're both smiling, Mama."

As Mrs. Provines took in the scene Magdelena described, they grinned at each other and raised their eyebrows. Ten feet further down the table, David Royer also spied the couple and scowled.

Aware of the many eyes that followed their ascent to the gathering, Samuel gave Sarah half of the bunch of Deadly Nightshade and they parted to join their respective families.

Meeting David's sullen stare, Samuel simply smiled. Then he sped in the direction of the muffled giggles on the other side of the table and rousted Susan and Rebecca from hiding. They all shared a most-knowing smirk.

"It's about time, Sarah," her mother said with exaggerated ire. "Finish up here while I tend to Leah. Looks like you found more than Deadly Nightshade on your little quest, didn't you?"

"Maybe, Mama," she replied blushing. "Maybe."

-13-

Corn Shucking Party

Three weeks had passed since Susan and Rebecca had accomplished their scheme to put Samuel and Sarah Provines in close company at Sunday meeting. The search for the healing Deadly Nightshade had succeeded in bringing the young sweethearts together in those stolen moments away from the watchful eyes of family and neighbors. Perhaps the spell of the forget-me-nots had helped – it certainly had not hurt the desired outcome, and Rebecca so enjoyed thinking it was magic. The girls caught the fond glimpses Samuel and Sarah had exchanged as their families' wagons pulled away in opposite directions from the Lesher farm.

Since that day Samuel had hummed quietly to himself and ignored the harshness in David's commands. Rebecca had even caught him when he thought no one was watching as he gazed west toward Waynesburg where Sarah would be helping out at her father's store.

Speculation about their favorite brother's romance had become a nightly preoccupation. Rebecca couldn't wait to revisit the preferred topic of their private conversation before falling asleep.

As they climbed the stairs to the loft that night Rebecca asked, "Did you notice how much earlier the sun is setting now, Susan?"

"Yes. And I'm afraid that even the heavy coverlet Mama gave us last week won't keep out the chill tonight," Susan added. The girls hushed their voices so as not to disturb Polly and Elizabeth who were already asleep in the next bed. They were exhausted after a rigorous day of making apple butter, their muscles aching from hours of stirring the thick, sweet mixture over a hot kettle.

"For somebody who is still scratching his rash, Samuel is in an awfully good mood these days," Susan whispered when they were snuggled under the woven blanket. "Did you see the twinkle in his eye when Papa mentioned that someone needed to go to town for more barrels and a new bucket?"

"Yes," said Rebecca. "I just hope Samuel thinks all the itching was worth it." They burst into giggles.

"Quiet down girls. You'll wake your sisters," their mother called from the room below. "You need your sleep. Tomorrow will be a busy day."

Indeed, thought Susan, mentally running down the list of chores they must complete before everyone arrived for the corn husking party. We'll see what tomorrow brings.

Everyone was up before the sun to help prepare food for the more than 80 friends and neighbors who would come to their barn to shuck a mountain of corn later that day. Rebecca noticed the barnyard cat on the stoop was washing its face with one white-mittened paw. As she  wrapped her shawl around her shoulders on her way to gather eggs from the hens, she thought, *The old superstition is right. Visitors are coming. How did the cat know?*

Weeks before, the whole family, with the help of the hired mill and tannery workers, had cut the plentiful corn stalks with large scythes and tied the sheaves into tall scratchy shocks that dotted the newly-stripped fields. It was backbreaking work and the girls had run themselves ragged fetching ladles of cool drinks for the men and helping them to tie the rough twine. The bundles allowed the corn to dry in the last of the autumn sunshine and gave the field mice the mistaken impression that they had found cozy winter homes with a ready supply of corn on the cob.

As the men tipped the shocks over to move them to the barn floor where everyone would soon gather, the resident mice ran for their lives, indignant at being so rudely evicted. Mukki gleefully gave chase as the mice made their frantic escape across the furrows. Her excited barking stopped only when she caught one and shook it ferociously before letting it thump to the ground as limp as one of the Susan's handmade rag dolls.

The Royers, as hosts of this corn shucking party, were expected to have all the corn on the barn floor ready for the festive gathering that transformed the otherwise tedious task into fun. The happy chatter of friends, bits of gossip, cider and food, and the likelihood of a fiddler, courtesy of their Scotch-Irish neighbors, would make the time and work fly by.

'Many hands make the work light,' Mama always told them. In just a very few hours of collective labor, all of the farmstead's corn could be shucked and the husks stripped from the cob. Although pride surely a sin, various families quietly remarked on their ability to husk the most corn in the shortest time. The young men were particularly eager to show off their skill and speed in the hope that they would be the first to find the solitary red ear of corn that had been hidden somewhere in the towering pile.

The fortunate fellow who found the red cob could kiss the girl of his choosing. All the girls on the other side of the barn harbored the fervent wish that the young man they fancied would be the one to find the prized red ear and bestow the coveted kiss. Many quiet tears were shed when the hoped-for kiss landed on some other girl's cheek. 'Who kissed who' would be the subject of conversation, consternation and speculation over many a winter hearth.

Tonight will be even more exciting, especially if Samuel gets lucky and Sarah gets the kiss, thought Rebecca as she and Susan set out the seven sweets and seven sours – dishes ranging from teeth-achingly sweet cabbage slaws to lip-puckering pickles – that were part of every respectable Pennsylvania German feast. Mother was unusually sharp in her instructions and fretted about the smallest detail.

The Royers, as owners of not only the most prosperous farmstead around, but a thriving mill and bustling tannery as well, were expected to offer their guests more than the usual fare in exchange for the work of husking acres of corn. Catherine, as mistress of the house, was responsible for their family's hospitality and she would brook no criticism from neighbors who were known to count and comment on the number and richness of the dishes offered at any gathering.

Diligent Elizabeth had been in charge of baking 50 loaves of bread for the day. The eyes of many of their guests would surely grow wide when they saw the stacks of delicate *wais bröd* on the wooden trays instead of the dark, grainy *shwarts bröd* that most everyone ate. White bread was not a treat for a household with a gristmill, but a luxury for many of their guests.

As a community, they could accomplish in a single evening what would take one farm family a week of relentless labor to achieve. By custom, the host family provided food and refreshment and a day of labor was expected in return. Although the Royers could not always participate in their neighbors' corn husking parties, no one failed to come to one of theirs.

Throughout all of the preparations, everyone in the family noticed the strain between David and Samuel. If David was in the tannery, Samuel went to the mill. When David went to the mill to help replace a cracked millstone, Samuel stayed to help David lift the heavy grinding disk, but quickly excused himself to check on a hobbled ox. It had been all they could do to be civil to each other even at family prayer the night before. Although eyes were supposed to be closed during devotions, Rebecca had noticed through her eyelashes that even Papa, like her, had broken the custom and glared sternly at his two warring sons even as he thanked God for the love of family.

'I don't know what to do about those two,' Susan overheard Mama say to Papa after everyone dispersed at the final Amen. 'It hasn't been right between them since Sunday service at Leshers.'

'Leave them alone,' Daniel had replied. 'They'll work out what needs working out.'

The earliest of the arrivals for the corn shucking pulled up to the barn just as the clear sky blushed with the pale pinks and blood reds of sunset. One wagon was followed by another and then another, the grunting of the teams of oxen and the neighing of horses signaling everyone's arrival. The Provines' sturdy wagon was among the first to arrive. Catherine, busy with the last of the apple dumplings, directed Cate to see how many guests had assembled. Cate darted into the yard to take a count, but was back in a flash. "Oh Mama, all of Nature is here and more!"

The hum of greetings and happy conversation soon filled the barn. Men and boys took their places on one side of the threshing floor and the women and girls stood opposite. They could hardly see one another over the mound of corn waiting to be shucked. The newest curiosity for those gathered was the frail young girl seated beside Connor McBride. She appeared to weigh less than a sack of potatoes and Connor took great pleasure in ordering her to refill his tankard and fetch his chewing tobacco. Very few who noticed his attitude appreciated his arrogance, but they opted to keep to their own business as the excitement mounted.

Amos Fahnestock stood up on one of the stacks of hay bales on the perimeter of the anxious contestants. "Mr. Royer is busy helping his wife set a second keg of cider for the meal, so he has asked me to ring the bell to start the husking." He smiled at the circle of young men ready to attack the waiting mound. "Are you ready?"

They all nodded and eyed each other in challenge.

"*Gut*," he announced. "On your mark – get set – go!" He clanged the bell and the highly anticipated husking began.

In no time at all the pile diminished like sand through a giant hourglass. The younger men pressed closer to the center ripping through the tough husks and flinging the exposed ears over their shoulders. Shouts of encouragement, laughter and exclamation echoed in the cavernous barn as clouds of corn silk floated in the crisp air. David and Samuel and the other German Baptist farmers looked odd without their hats. The straight line separating the red and white of their foreheads marked where the brims had shielded their faces from the blazing sun. All of the young men attacked each ear in a frenzy, oblivious to the husks' sharp edges as they stripped the corn of its brittle

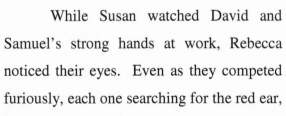

sheaths. *We'll need lots of Mama's sage hand salve come morning*, Susan thought.

While Susan watched David and Samuel's strong hands at work, Rebecca noticed their eyes. Even as they competed furiously, each one searching for the red ear, they both kept a careful check on Sarah Provines, who sat off to the side haphazardly tugging on the dry casings of the corn.

Surely she must feel the heat of their stares, thought Rebecca, who shivered at the intensity of their intermittent gazes. Trouble was brewing as surely as the chicory coffee that was boiling in the large pot outside.

No sooner had this unsettling thought come to her, than a great shout rang out and all eyes turned to Samuel who raised the red ear in triumph! Susan gave Rebecca's hand a conspiratorial squeeze.

As Samuel rose to approach Sarah, the crowd watched in horror as he tripped over David's outstretched foot. Samuel fell to his knees and the red ear flew up in the air, nearly striking the barn's main chestnut beam. As it plummeted to earth, David reached out and seized it. Everyone gasped. They all knew that David would not have dared to do such a despicable thing if his father were present. Likewise, they knew better than to inform on him and spoil the celebration. Daniel's temper was well known.

In less time than it took a cricket to chirp, David confronted Sarah and planted a rough kiss on the startled girl's lips.

Some more raucous observers whooped, but Rebecca and Susan detected distinct, if subtle, disapproval in the murmur of the rest of crowd as they watched Samuel glower helplessly. Sarah's pretty pink cheeks burned with a rosy mixture of embarrassment and anger.

David, his chest puffed out against his straining suspenders, was oblivious to the disapproval as he slapped George Schmucker on the back and headed outside to the wooden tables groaning under the weight of platters of venison, pork and squab.

"Good catch," said George with little conviction as David stomped by.

"Why, yes, George, she is – a very good catch indeed!" David laughed.

The bell rang a second time – the call to come to the feast. Thankful for a diversion that would break the tension, the folks brushed off their dusty, corn silk-covered clothes and moved for the tables. As the final debris of the competition settled to the ground, Samuel lingered in the barn to quiet his breathing – and his soul. He had lost his appetite. He was the last to leave to get his meal, but was not about to let David out of his sight for long. Not while Sarah was nearby.

The crowd regained its carefree attitude as they partook of the bounty offered at the serving tables. From his place at the end of the line, Samuel did his best to ignore David rather than spoil the festivities for his family and their guests. However, his anger overcame his best intentions when he overheard David remark to Sean McBride with a smug chuckle, "Why she's the best catch since I hooked that huge trout last year."

David no sooner turned to the table to serve up a hearty helping of sauerkraut than Samuel broke ranks and marched directly up to him. Sean quickly stepped aside as others close by hushed at the renewed conflict. In the growing dusk, Rebecca could almost see the sparks fly between them.

"'Tis a sin, brother, to take that which is not yours," Samuel muttered through clenched teeth.

David stood to confront him. "What are you talking about, little brother? I got the red ear and the kiss. And as your older brother, I'll be the first to marry as well. Sarah's a comely girl with hips wide enough to bear strong sons. She will make someone, most likely me, a fine wife."

Out of respect for their hosts, none of the diners intervened in the continued display of fraternal hostility, but everyone at the meal soon became aware of the two strapping brothers leaning menacingly toward one another.

Samuel secured his ground in the face of David's increased gloating. "She is, indeed, all that you say, Brother, but she'll be no wife of yours, if I can do anything about it."

"As if you *could* do anything about it, Samuel," said David towering over his slimmer, younger brother. "I am the eldest son. What can you offer a girl like Sarah? I'll have the tannery and the mill and be tax collector like Papa one day. I will do the first choosing. Go find yourself another girl."

"I'll not have another, David," Samuel declared as much to himself as to his brother. "Sarah has already shown a fondness for me and has no regard for your ugly manners and angry ways."

"The two of you have spoken of this?" roared David wide-eyed. "You had no right!" He spit out the words, pressing the full weight of his shoulder against Samuel's chest.

"This will stop now!" boomed a voice from the crowd. Both men straightened at the sound of their father's voice. "We do not air our differences in front of others, particularly those who do not share our ways," Daniel hissed, tilting his chin in the direction of the McBrides, Burns, McKendricks and other 'English' families standing outside the barn doors. Even the fiddlers were eyeing the two brothers from a distance as they rosined their bows. "We will discuss this in the morning."

The brothers traded one last glare and parted, giving each other neutral ground. David stormed away and Samuel returned to his place at the end of the line. Slowly, the previous din of activity returned.

Nearly an hour later, the feasting ended and the music began. Although the Royers and like-minded German Dunkards did not approve of dancing, no one else could resist the lively music. They watched their Scotch-Irish neighbors do reels and jigs on the newly-swept floorboards. Samuel, knowing David had left the barn, threaded his way through the crowd to Sarah's side, his hooded glances silently expressing his sympathy and dismay. With so many eyes on them, Sarah's stony expression gave nothing away. Samuel sat calmly beside her, but dared not even touch her hand in public. As much as both of them may have wanted to comfort the other, that was for another time, a more proper time. Samuel had determined in his own mind that he would finally act on his feelings. As soon as possible, he would speak to Mr. Provines and then ask Sarah to be his wife.

David did not return to the barn where the women's voices and children's playful shrieks reminded him of a gaggle of geese. Instead, he found consolation in the company of the older men, some smoking clay pipes and sipping whiskey, outside the barn.

"Not to worry, son," slurred Sean McBride's father Silas who had shucked more whiskey than corn that day. "There be more maids where she's come from."

David kicked over the nearby spittoon. "If I can't have that one, I'll have no wife at all." He stalked off into the darkness.

-14-

Everything but the Squeal

Rebecca crouched under her coarse, woolen cape behind the cabin with her eyes closed and hands clamped over her ears. The squeals and grunts of the hogs being herded to slaughter was more than she could stand. Susan sat patiently beside her with an arm resting on her sister's shoulder. "I know it's nasty business, Rebecca, but try to think about the delicious crisp bacon and smoke-cured ham."

"They really do taste wonderful, Susan, but . . ."

"Bam!" Rebecca's cowering body jerked at the report of her father's rifle, just as she had at the six previous shots that morning. Remembering past years, she had fled to her hiding place immediately after she helped to clean up the huge pre-dawn breakfast for all of the participants in the big day.

"I think that's the last one," said Susan. "No more killing or squealing at least. Why don't you go in and help Mama. She's got to have nearly a ton of food ready by noon. By then the men will have finished their part of the butcherin' and be well into their shooting matches and heaving shoulder stones. There are five families of mouths to feed today."

Rebecca scurried away slipping a bit on the late-November frost that had escaped the sun in the shadow of the cabin. Susan rubbed her hands together to warm them and ventured behind the barn for a peek at the on-going activities before she, too, took her station in the kitchen.

The roaring outside fires cast an orange glow on the steam that poured from the tops of the immense hogshead barrels full of scalding water. David and Laban Wingert were directing the mule and pulley system rigged to a nearby tree to lower a hefty, strung carcass into one vat, while Silas  McBride was laboring to lift another hog in a similar fashion from the other. Each hog weighed nearly 300 pounds. Samuel stood near Silas with his broad knife scraping the hair and bristles that the scalding water had loosened from the hog's skin as the carcass emerged from the barrel.

As Silas stepped aside, Sean McBride slit the throat from front to back, and then he and Samuel together twisted the neck until the backbone broke and the head separated. They tossed the severed skull into a nearby kettle.

Sean grabbed hold of the drooping tongue. "Just think of the scrumptious meal this will make," he said.

The brains would be fried in lard for a tasty meal and the rest of head meat would be used for mincemeat, headcheese, puddin' and more. Every part of the sacrificed beasts would be used.

After the beheading, the pulley swung the body away from the hogshead toward waiting makeshift tables of boards and sawhorses. While still suspended, the belly was sliced open with an ax and sharp knife with the men being careful not to nick the intestines that were tied off and scooped out into a large bucket. The women would strip and clean them later for sausage casings to be stuffed with meat trimmings and fat ground together in the sausage mill and seasoned. The last thing before lowering the hogs to the tables was to saw through the backbone.

Just behind them, the tables strained under the weight of six more porcine bodies that lay spread-eagle on their backs in various stages of being cut into their essential parts by yet more men. Hams from the hindquarters, shoulders for salt pork from the front quarters, and bacon from between the two were piled high waiting to be salted and smoked. John and Jacob were sawing vigorously through the leg bones in a race to see who could accumulate the largest pile of pig feet for pickling in small crocks.

The chill November air lay heavy atop a thick, warm cloud that encompassed the barnyard. The humidity and stench of the slaughter coated the men's noses and mouths as they breathed heavily at their various jobs. Susan hated the butchery nearly as much as her sister. She retreated from the morbid fog that grew more dense as the work intensified. Making her way to the cabin, she gave silent thanks that she was not born a boy who had to be a part of such killing.

All that remained of the seven animals would be waiting after the noon meal so that the women could begin their contribution to the butchering. A sizable portion would be set aside for the traditional *metzel-sup* for Widow Funk. Life was exceptionally difficult for a woman who had lost the strong arms of her husband and the community welcomed the opportunity to help. Nothing – from the snout to the tail – would be wasted. Like Omah Royer used to say, "We use everything but the squeal."

As the fires died under the steaming hogsheads and all of the salt pork and hams were suspended from the smokehouse hooks, the laboring men moved on to the "friendly" contests for the day.

"Whoa, Samuel. You missed that target by a mile. Must be thinking about that sweet girl of yours, huh?" said George Schmucker. The tannery workers had been released from their usual tasks to help with the butchering and enjoy a few welcome hours of spirited competition.

"Let me have a go now," said David reaching for the family's Pennsylvania rifle in Samuel's hands. "That bulls-eye should be easier to hit than a whitetail buck at ten yards." He relished every opportunity to outmatch his younger brother since the engagement between Sarah and Samuel was approved and would be properly announced at the appropriate Sunday meeting. No one was anxious to recall the past romantic rivalry between the young men – or, if they did, they kept silent, knowing well the elder brother's temperament. As for David, his knowledge alone of his loss was enough to gall him every time he saw his younger brother smile. He took careful aim at the target, as each man had only one shot. Ammunition was too expensive to waste on games.

"Bam!"

David smirked as a hole appeared just inches off the center mark painted on the hay bale. "Better to be a bachelor with good aim than a husband with no venison on the table." He handed the rifle back to Samuel.

"But it takes an able woman to make the venison tasty," said George.

"Right you are, laddie," laughed Connor McBride, a little into his cups having indulged in more than his usual swig of corn liquor after hard labor. He was much like his father in that regard.

"And they spice up even more than that, if you get the right one. Know what I mean?" He elbowed Daniel and winked.

Daniel tightened his lips. It was pretty common knowledge that Connor had little compassion for his fragile new bride Maggie. The rumor was that she was already with child, though she was but a girl herself and had barely survived her childhood years. Everyone knew that Maggie had lived in the poorhouse on the east side of town with her father, an itinerant farmhand who loved whiskey more than his family. The poorhouse was little more than an abandoned shack, so Maggie's life with Connor, though still miserable, at least afforded her food and more adequate shelter.

"Enough of that, Connor," Daniel said. "By the end of this day, those good women cooking up dinner right now will have worked every bit as hard as any man here. I don't know a lick about making the sausage and scrapple that we had for breakfast this morning, but I sure do enjoy eating it."

"Right," added Amos Fahnestock slapping Josiah Lehman on the back. "And your Rachael knows just how much sage and honey and such to add to the pork and fat of the sausage before stuffing it to make a man's mouth water just at the thought of it."

David turned a deaf ear to the conversation.

"I hear your Papa has seen fit to set you and Sarah on a prime ten acres that borders our place," Amos said to Samuel. "I can't think of better neighbors. Have you begun work on a cabin yet?"

"Thank you, Mr. Fahnestock. I've split some sizeable logs and stacked them near the site. The plot strings are in place. I hope to be inviting lots of you to a cabin-raising as soon as the weather breaks in February – before spring planting."

"Maybe the rest of your family will be ready to move into their fine, new stone house over there by then." He indicated the nearby construction that was thankfully under roof before the first snowfall.

"We'll be there when you need us, Samuel," offered George who stood nearby. "What's say we get our muscles primed for heaving your rafters and walls right now? I see you've gathered an impressive collection of stones over by the smokehouse. Let's see who can heave one the farthest. The dinner bell will soon be ringin'."

As the challenge spread, the group made their way toward the back of the smokehouse. David maneuvered himself beside Samuel. "Next time we go to gather lumber for the tannery, I'll put aside some of the longer, straighter hardwood trunks for your project," he mentioned offhandedly.

Samuel tugged on his brother's elbow to command his attention. "Thank you, Brother. I'll count on you to help me make it a strong home." Samuel extended his hand.

David hesitated just a beat and then returned the gesture. After they shook hands, David nodded and moved away to catch up with the rest of the men. Perhaps there could finally be peace between the two.

Remnants of the day's feast littered the large table. All that remained were the apple crumb pies and turnovers waiting beside pitchers of steaming cider. Polly lifted the platter holding the knobby bone of a once prodigious ham to make space for the crock of sweet cream some would pour on their chosen dessert.

"I can't believe we ate that entire ham," she said. "Especially with all the turnips and mounds of *shnitz un knep* – even if we did have to use salt pork to make it. It's been too long since we had the taste of fresh pork. I can't wait until today's hogs are ready for the table."

As she made to leave, Samuel caught Polly's sleeve. "That ham we ate was almost as big as the boulder George flung today. He outdid everyone else by at least an arm's length." He watched for her reaction knowing full well that George had not missed a move she had made all day.

She hesitated. "Show her those muscles, George," he teased. George shook his head and quickly studied his slice of pie.

Polly glanced at George and blushed, but moved away objecting almost too much. "Mules are strong, too, but who wants to look at them?"

"Whoa!" hooted a number of men at the table as Polly marched toward the kitchen.

Catherine turned around at the chorus. "Why all the ruckus?" No one responded, but it was hard to miss George's red face and Polly's agitation.

Catherine pondered to herself and sighed, *May soon be another one wants to leave the nest. Where has the time flown, Lord? But I suspect that Polly's blush is as much from affection for George as embarrassment. I suppose I must alert Daniel, though I'm sure it won't be pleasant news for him that one of his daughters has taken a fancy to one of his tannery workers.* She stole a quick look at George. *Although he has a fine shock of rusty brown curls.* She smiled in spite of herself until her original doubts returned. *I just wish it could be as easy a match for Daniel as was Samuel's to Sarah, but I fear it won't be.*

Susanna Fahnestock broke Catherine's musing as she passed by balancing an armful of dirty plates.

"Just scrape the leavings into that old slop bucket in the corner. It'll help to start to fatten the next generation of potential pigs," Catherine said.

Susanna nodded and smiled. "I've got plenty of sweet sage and pepper to season the sausage. Before you know it, I'll be elbow deep in raw meat instead of scraps, and Martha and Prudence will be busy funneling it into the casings."

"You always make it so tasty." Catherine pointed behind her. "And I've got my Mama's sassafras lard stick to stir the rendering kettle. Seems to take forever until the fat has cooked down to those crispy brown cracklin's that float on top. The girls can lift them off with strainers. They make good munching. Then we can scoop out the creamy, white lard into all of those empty crocks that need to be refilled for another year. With 12 to feed, plus the hired help, I nearly ran out this year."

Rachael sat nearby finishing her dessert and listening to the conversation. She shook her head. "I don't know how you do it, Mrs. Royer. I don't have enough hours in the day to handle my six, much less ten."

"The older children are wonderful help, but you're right, Mrs. Lehman. The old adage is true. 'Men work from dawn til' setting sun, but women's work is never done.'"

Then, as master of the kitchen she announced, "Gentlemen, after you've enjoyed your dessert, get busy with setting up the tables and kettles so we women can be at our work as soon as everything is cleared. Be careful with the salt barrels. You know it's as precious as gold. We'll need every grain if we want to be keeping the bulk of that meat fit for the table this year and cabbage has been extra plentiful this season for sauerkraut. Wouldn't hurt to double-check the smokehouse, too. Make sure it's ready to be stuffed and sealed up tight with a good stock of hickory embers doing their job. Set the kettles on the fire to render the lard and stand up the crocks right beside for easy dipping."

"This is not our first butcherin', wife," Daniel said. "We'll be about our duties and hope to complete them as well as you have this delicious meal." The others added to the compliment. "Now," he continued, "let us all give thanks to the Lord again for the bounty of this day."

Even tipsy Silas McBride was caught up in the spirit and observed the moment of spontaneous silence for personal prayers that followed. Daniel pronounced the final Amen and the wheels of the day's activities again began to turn. The leaden fog was lifting from the barnyard to reveal a gray horizon – some called it a 'snow sky.' A premature taste of winter could soon reveal part of its wonder.

The exciting yet exhausting day collected its toll as the tired Royer clan, the young and the not-so-young, fell into bed that night. Below the cold whisper of the light wind through the cracks in between the roof eaves and the floor of their loft, Susan detected a muffled whimper. It was coming from Polly's sleeping pallet. Being careful not to arouse the other girls, Susan made her way toward the mournful sound. Polly jumped slightly when she sensed Susan's approach and immediately ceased her weeping.

"Polly, what's wrong? Why are you crying?" asked Susan.

"Oh, Susan." Polly grabbed Susan's hand and squeezed. "I'm so ashamed of myself and . . . and scared."

"Ashamed? Scared? But why, Polly? What are you talking about?" Susan grasped Polly's hand between both of hers for comfort.

"All the talk of Samuel and Sarah's cabin and . . . and marriage. Oh, Susan, I want so much to be happy for them. Really I do, but . . . but it just makes me scared to think that George and I may never . . . that Papa will never . . ."

Susan snuggled in beside Polly and hugged her. She could think of nothing honest to say about Papa's attitude to allay her sister's fears. All she could do was hold on to her and love her. "I'm sure Samuel and Sarah didn't notice, and if Samuel did, I just know he would understand. Try to sleep now. We never know what tomorrow might bring – what God might provide."

Doubly fatigued by both the physical and emotional demands of the day, Polly's breathing soon eased and her body drooped with sleep. Susan made her way back to her place beside Cate.

Poor Polly, she thought. *What will she and George do, I wonder?*

Now, it would be hard for Susan to sleep.

-15-

Scary Stories by the Fire

Rebecca was miserable. The change in the weather always made her sick. She had just adjusted to the sharp cold winter when summer's warmth returned suddenly out of season. Her swollen throat felt as though it was sprinkled with ground glass. All day long, even in the sticky sunshine as she gathered the last of the vegetables from the garden, her handkerchief had been her constant companion. No sooner did she tuck it into her apron pocket than she had to pull it out to capture the ceaseless dripping of her now-reddened nose.

"Don't complain so," said Polly when Rebecca had moaned about her unexpected sneeze in the garden that afternoon that scattered all of the lettuce seeds she had carefully gathered in her apron for next year's crop. In a wave of frustration she had kicked her gathering basket across the center path sending the knotty gourds flying everywhere.

"Making a fuss won't make you better," said Susan, who was harvesting late heads of cabbage. "Everyone catches colds in Indian Summer. You'll be fine."

137

But by evening, Rebecca's cough had attracted her mother's unwelcome attention, prompting the medicinal poultice that now hugged her chest. Rebecca wondered if this new misery of the cure was worse than the sniffles and the painful hacking of her ailment that echoed through the two rooms on the main level of the house.

Seated by the hearth, Daniel put down the copy of the *Hager's-town Almanack* that he was consulting for recommended planting times. He gave Rebecca an appraising glance. "Come sit closer to the fire, *Liebchen*," he said with a rare softness.

The cabin was so quiet she could hear the crackle of the fire as the household settled in for evening chores. Her brother David was reviewing accounts at the table by candlelight, while Samuel mended leather harnesses by the lantern's glow outside the cabin door. Susan was combing the burrs out of Mukki's fur as Nan softly chewed on a knotted cloth in the cradle.

Polly had chosen a seat a few feet away from the others. She had replaced the usual sampler in her embroidery hoop with a plain linsey-woolsey handkerchief. One corner of the cloth dangled from the edge of the loop toward Polly to conceal a tiny "G S" of blue thread near the hem. She didn't want to risk being discovered as she added the final stitches to the heart that framed the tiny pink "P R" in the opposite corner of the handkerchief to complete her gift for George.

Rebecca tried to take her mind off the offensive packet treating her cold – its pungent fumes made her nose crinkle – by recalling her earlier conversation with Polly in the garden. "Papa, why is this time of year called Indian Summer?"

"I know! I know!" Susan called from across the room. "It's because the leaves are turning such beautiful bright colors, like the reds and yellows of Indian beads and blankets."

"Oh, no, that's not it at all," declared Polly. "It's because this is the time of year when the Indians always gathered in the last of the summer corn."

"Those are both good ideas," said Daniel tugging on his beard. Rebecca was close enough to see a strand or two of silver. "But the real reason we call this last stretch of warm weather before winter "Indian Summer" isn't nearly so pleasant. Let me explain. This was a wild country when your great-grandfather Sebastian Royer first came here from the Rhineland more than 90 years ago. No open fields or fenced gardens or animals grazing peacefully. The land here was only a dense, dark and dangerous forest filled with wild boar, bears, beaver, deer, a few settlers and, of course, savage Indians."

"Savage," Rebecca repeated softly. Frightening images of bloodthirsty warriors from stories she had heard came to mind, even though she had never seen an Indian in her life. She became so distressed she scooted closer to her father's side forgetting about the smelly camphor plaster resting on her chest. The sound of the packet falling to the floor startled her mother, who stopped her spinning by the fireplace.

"Now Daniel, do not get the children stirred up right before bed. We want them to have sweet dreams."

Rebecca sheepishly gathered the poultice to her chest and resumed her seat nearer her father.

"You're right, Catherine. It is late and they wouldn't be interested anyway," he said with a hint of teasing in his tone.

"What?" cried Rebecca, Susan and Polly in chorus.

"Well, I guess you can continue, Daniel." Catherine shook her head and smiled, thinking it was good for her husband to let their children see his more tender side. "But when the wind howls through the rafters tonight, I don't want you girls thinking Indians are attacking."

"And best not be waking us up in the middle of the night with your crying if you do," added Daniel with an exaggerated grunt.

Their parents' warnings were not groundless. Rebecca had been troubled by nightmares before, but it was the stories her mother had told about why their ancestors had come to the New World from the Rhineland and Switzerland that terrified her.

Tonight, her father had skipped over the real reason her great-grandfather originally came to America. As her mother had once explained, if her grandfather had stayed in Europe, he would have been killed for his belief that only adults should be baptized in the church. He and fellow Anabaptists had fled the persecution that sent many others to horrible deaths. They had been forced to leave because, in her Mama's words 'People in power persecuted them for what they believed.' Many of the Anabaptists had been burned at the stake or drowned for believing that only reasoning adults and not helpless infants could freely accept the gifts of heaven.

Rebecca had always been confounded by the idea that Christians, who are supposed to love one another, could kill fellow Christians over something as trivial as whether they were baptized as babies or adults.

As if the good Lord would choose one way of accepting his grace over another, thought Rebecca. *I'll never understand how people could be so awful.*

"Now, where was I?" Daniel said.

"You were telling us about savage Indians and Indian Summer," Susan reminded him gently.

"Oh yes, and the poor little Renfrew sisters."

"But that's just a tale Opah used to tell," said Catherine cautioning her husband with a raised eyebrow.

"Yes, but the story is true," said Daniel. "It happened when your Opah was a very young man and the English were fighting against the French and their Indian allies over control of this very territory. The Indians took advantage of the few weeks of warmer weather in the autumn to raid the farms that produced grain for the British soldiers' horses. As the farmers were harvesting the last of their crops, the Indians would attack, often tomahawking and scalping entire families. Hence the term Indian Summer."

"Oh," the girls whispered.

"You children know from your own work in the fields that you can't harvest crops and hold a rifle at the same time," Daniel reminded them. "The Indian raiders often watched a farmstead for days and waited until the farmer got to the far end of the field away from his firearm before they attacked. With the farmer dead, his family was left unprotected. The French and their Indian friends reasoned rightly that by destroying the food supply for the horses, the English soldiers couldn't defend anyone on the frontier. Many of the families around here fled north to Carlisle for safety, abandoning their farms. This made the French and their Indian friends happy because they didn't want the English, German, or Scotch-Irish settlers living in this beautiful valley. They wanted all of us to go back where we came from.

"That's why poor little Jane and Sarah Renfrew were killed," said Daniel with a sigh. "Their family had come from Scotland to farm and build a new life. The girls were washing clothes down by the creek, not far from where Polly found the wild blackberries last summer. That's where the Indians murdered the innocents and took their scalps."

Rebecca cringed at the word scalps.

"But Papa, why did they have to kill them?" she asked.

"Don't be so silly," scoffed Susan, having abandoned Mukki's tangled coat in favor of her embroidery hoop. "That's what most Indians do."

"Who can explain the cruelty of one to another?" said Daniel. "But within days, local hunters tracked those Indians over the Tuscarora Mountains west of here. When the Indians stopped to feast on wild plums, the men attacked. They killed the two Indians and brought the girls' scalps back in time to be buried with their bodies."

For as long as they could remember Rebecca and Susan had known that the two Renfrew girls were buried near the creek not far from where they had been murdered. Sean

143

McBride once pointed out what he claimed was the exact spot. "You can tell by the red in the soil," he said as he teased them about the murdered girls' ghosts coming after them. Sensible Elizabeth had told them to never mind such foolishness, but Sean's menacing laughter had stayed with Rebecca.

From that day on, neither she nor Susan liked being on the east side of the creek. Sometimes the livestock would wander that way in search of sweet moss. Papa would order them to fetch the stray cows from the edge of the water. Rebecca always obeyed, but shuddered at the thought of possibly stepping on top of the little girls' lonely graves.

"It's off to bed with you," Catherine insisted setting aside her hand spindle and skein of flax thread.

"Mama," said Rebecca as she shuffled toward the loft. "I don't think the nice warm days of Indian Summer will be as nice anymore. Not since Papa's story."

Catherine hugged her. "The Lord sends us beautiful things like warm Indian Summer days. It is right that we enjoy them. Sleep tight, *Liebling*."

Once in bed, Rebecca's coughing subsided. Either the poultice worked or she was simply exhausted.

The next morning the sun was bright, but the light frost that made everything sparkle and the grass crunch under her leather soles told her that the onset of winter had returned.

Catherine sent her to the creek after breakfast to look for hickory nuts that she wanted to use in her bread. Rebecca didn't protest. It was better to mind Mama than face Papa if you challenged a chore. Rebecca wanted to be a good helper, but her mother was sending her to the very area where the Renfrew sisters had been killed. Rebecca was mindful of her father's words from the night before as she lifted the hem of her skirt and pushed her way through the bramble toward the sound of the rushing water.

Hickory nuts were scarce, but Rebecca knew she could not return to the cabin empty-handed. Polly never missed the chance to advise in her oh-so-smarter-than-you-are tone of voice, 'What you are searching for is almost always in front of you if you will take the time to look.' Her older sister smugly imparted this wisdom every time Rebecca dropped a sewing needle or Mama misplaced her spectacles.

Suddenly, a noise in the brush startled Rebecca. The snap of twigs told her she was not alone. She spun around and saw them. Two men with dark, weathered faces, one with feathers in his hair, were only 20 feet away pulling a canvas-covered cart.

Gott in Himmel, she cried to herself for fear had stolen her voice. *I'm going to be scalped!*

Frantic, Rebecca turned and ran away as fast as she could, ripping her sleeve on the thorn of a wild locust tree. The jagged scratch hurt and she would be scolded for the large tear in her garment, but that didn't matter now. Somehow she had to tell Papa and her brothers that they were about to be attacked, but no one would hear her over the sound of the grinding stones at the mill and the beating of the hides in the tannery.

As she picked up speed in the clearing and hurtled toward the mill, she thought of the clay bird whistle hidden safely in her pocket. Without missing a step, she put it to her lips and blew as hard as she could. From its beak came a shrill so loud that it hurt her ears. Heartened by the noise, she ran even faster along the millrace and was relieved to see the men stop their work to see what made her run so.

"Stop that infernal noise!" David shouted as he charged up the hill from the tannery.

"What's wrong, little one?" Samuel called running up from the mill. He crouched down to receive her into his open arms. She threw herself against his chest.

"Indians! Indians!" she blurted between painful gasps.

The six men, wiping sweat from their brows even in the chill morning air, looked at her stunned and then did the last thing she ever would have expected. They all laughed. Even Samuel.

Above her confusion and disbelief, she heard David, who rarely so much as grinned, laughing so loud that she jumped even higher than when she first glimpsed the Indians. *"Kleine Dummkopf,"* he said. "There are no Indians around here anymore!"

Angry and frustrated by their refusal to believe her, Rebecca collapsed in tears. Samuel gently sat her on the ground in front of him. "There, there," he soothed. "Tell me what you saw."

Her face red with embarrassment and wet with tears, she stammered, "T . . . two men. Wa . . . one was surely an Indian. Th . . . they were coming up by the creek. They're headed this way, Samuel. We've got to warn everyone!" she pleaded.

"Did they have a cart with them?"

"Yes!" Her face brightened with hope her story would be confirmed.

"And was one wearing feathers in his hair?"

"Oh, yes, Samuel. You understand!"

"And are these the men?" he said pointing over her shoulder.

Afraid to look, but emboldened by Samuel's calm, Rebecca turned to see. Just behind her, making their way past the edge of the garden, were the very men who minutes before had startled her in the woods.

"Oh, *Schatzi,*" said Samuel, struggling to be serious. "It's just the tinker and his helper, come to sell Mama ribbons and tin wear."

Rebecca fell into his arms again, this time in shame, as Samuel patted her shoulder until the laughter of the others faded and they returned to their work.

For weeks to follow family members would pause in their daily tasks to ask Rebecca if she had seen any Indians lately. She always blushed and fumed with injured pride and flew to the garden or privy to escape their chuckling. She could hardly wait until the work of the final harvest and preparations for the snowy weather began. The painstaking task of preserving foods for the winter and putting the garden to bed would erase her embarrassing false alarm from everyone's mind.

Her only comfort was that in the midst of all the excitement, no one had asked her where she had gotten the whistle. She had safely hidden it away in the space under the floorboards beneath her rope bed. *My gift from John Bell should stay there awhile*, she thought, as she sat idly by the garden fence snapping off the heads of dead yarrow that her mother would brew into a soothing tea. *With a dollop of honey, the tea won't taste so bad*, she thought, smiling softly to herself.

-16-

Preserving the Bounty

T here," announced nearly six-year-old Cate displaying a length of parboiled green beans that she had strung together onto a strand of linen thread salvaged from the flax harvest. "One more string of leather britches for the rafters. That makes eight that I've finished today. Papa will have to sharpen my bone needle again."

"*Gut, meines Liebchen*," said Elizabeth who was methodically shelling the corn kernels from the pile of dried cobs stacked beside her stool. The nuggets would be bagged and used for hominy or ground for corn mush or bread.

A bountiful harvest meant not only delicious fresh vegetables and fruits for the table, but also considerable labor to preserve enough of the foodstuffs for the family to eat for the rest of the year – from after the frost did its damage until the new harvest. No sooner was a meal prepared and eaten than work was begun to preserve food for the many lean months to come.

Last winter, no snow had fallen on Christmas and the old saying 'Green Christmas. White Easter' had proven true. As the colder weather hung on, Elizabeth remembered the hint of panic in her mother's eyes back then when Cate had reported on the dwindling inventory of crocks and crates her mother had asked her to tally in late March. Cate was just learning her numbers and proud that her mother had given her this task. While none of the other family members noticed, Elizabeth was keenly aware that from that day on, when the family gathered around the table, the soup had more water added to it and the basket held fewer biscuits. Catherine would make certain that *this* year her family would be well fed until the spring began to offer new harvests.

Perhaps this winter would be kinder and grant Catherine more peace of mind, but the leanness of last year had left its mark. Though she tried to mask it, Elizabeth, for one, felt more urgency in her Mama's drive to over-stuff the larder for the coming winter.

The late autumn four-square garden was a patchwork of idle beds after the September harvest of ripened green beans, peas, cucumbers, cabbages and summer squash. The green beans and peas were dried by the air and sun, but cucumbers and cabbages were preserved in vinegar or salt baths. Pottery jars of pickles flavored with dill, and sometimes with a little honey as well, lined the kitchen shelves behind the ones that remained from earlier cucumber harvests. Larger six-gallon earthenware crocks of sauerkraut stood on the dirt floor beneath. Cate had especially enjoyed her role in the "kraut" preparation that required her to scrub her feet and stomp on the shredded cabbage in the largest of the crocks to break up the fibers before the salt was added to begin the brining process.

Most of the herbs that had filled the outside edges of the garden were hanging upside down in bundles from the rafters to dry. The green stalks of the root vegetables – the potatoes, turnips, carrots, and onions – that remained in the garden soil were beginning to shrivel and droop and soon would be dead enough to indicate it was time to bring out the shovels for digging.

Jacob had already carried a fresh bag of sawdust to the root cellar, a large cave-like storage area dug beneath the level of the dirt floor accessed through a musty, wood-framed panel in the far corner of the kitchen. The dusty potatoes, purple-topped turnips and orange carrots would keep there for months at the more constant cool temperature packed into crates of sawdust. Onions would dangle from the rafters on a string line alongside the green bean leather britches above the crocks of pickles, sauerkraut and ginger cookies that would be parceled out during the year.

"Actually, it's more fun to string up the cored apple slices," Cate said. "I don't need to use a needle and I get to eat the broken sections that can't be strung. They're tastier than green beans, for sure. I've finished 23 strings of apple rings already."

"And corn muffins taste soooo good when they soak up Mama's peach honey jam," added Rebecca as she stirred the large kettle of corn mush suspended from an iron hook just close enough to the fire to keep it warm, but not so close as to dry it out for evening supper. "And we've sealed up four jars for every one jar we've eaten since the peaches got ripe."

"It's just the best thing ever with warm cider on a really cold, gray winter day," said Susan closing her eyes to relish the memory as she added two more logs to the smoldering hearth.

"And those days are not far off," sighed Polly as she put some dried venison and pitchers of warm cider on the table and gazed out the side window of the log house at the sunset-streaked sky. "Just look how short the days are getting already."

Taking note of the time, Catherine advised her daughters, "Why don't you girls go ahead and eat your supper." Evening meals were much simpler and less structured than midday. "Your brothers will soon be pouring in the door famished. Polly's arms and spirit will be tired when she returns from candle-dipping at Frau Fahnestock's. The rest of us are best fed and out of the way."

"Hush, Polly," George whispered as they embraced in the shadow of the Fahnestock's small barn. They rocked gently knowing the risk they were taking, but unwilling to give up an opportunity to be together. Surely God would not forbid their love for each other. Surely He would let them be truly together one day. They took turns reassuring each other of this when uncertainty and guilt overcame them. They just needed to be patient and true to each other until their world was ready for them. Until then, these few forbidden meetings were all they had.

Polly calmed a bit and laid her hands on George's chest. Then she brushed his flushed cheek and curly, red hair. "But I miss you so. It's so hard to pretend I don't care about you when people are watching, but it would be even harder not to see you at all."

"It's hard for me too." He pulled the handkerchief she had embroidered for him from his pocket and wiped the tears from her cheeks. "Your handkerchief is always with me – a special part of you next to me. I wish it could be more, but it's not going to be like this forever. Papa promised that when I'm 18, next month, I can leave home and apprentice for Uncle

Cyrus in Waynesburg. Then I'll be able to talk to your papa. I can tell him I'll be able to take proper care of you."

"But what if Papa still says no? You know how he can be. You've seen his temper at the tannery." She hugged George hard. "I'm so afraid he won't approve. Then what will we do? With the brotherhood in such an uproar – all the tension between families, who knows what he'll say?"

"We'll deal with that when and if we have to. Whatever he says, I'll never leave you, Polly." He kissed her forehead. "Whatever it takes, we'll be together – always."

"Promise?"

"Do you really need to ask?"

"Yes, promise me. Promise me, George. As long as I can remember, Papa always gets his way, so you need to promise me he won't keep us apart."

George carefully folded the handkerchief, tucked it inside his shirt and held it next to his heart.

"I solemnly swear that nothing and no one will come between us." As the coral rays of the setting sun tinted the white of her bonnet, he lifted her chin and they kissed.

"Now, you'd better get moving. Your Mama knows Mrs. Fahnestock wouldn't be keeping you here to help her after dark."

Polly scooped up her basket of provisions for the family that Mrs. Fahnestock had given in exchange for Polly's help with candle-dipping. "Mama will be glad to see the bag of hazelnuts she sent along this time."

"And I'll be glad when it's next Tuesday – your day to help Mrs. Fahnestock again."

She grinned.

"Now there's the smile I fell in love with," George said. As they reluctantly parted, the dusk and trees hid them all too soon from each other's view.

As the girls ladled themselves some mush and settled at the table, Catherine looked over at Daniel seated at a small desk beside the downstairs sleeping alcove. He had left his manual labors early to give his attention to necessary paperwork for the household and tax collections. "Are you ready for supper, Husband?"

"I'll wait for the boys," he answered.

As if prompted, the next second John and Jacob's boots clomped onto the front porch and they began to pound the wooden boards in an attempt to loosen the dirt from the soles. They lumbered in the door covered with dried slip and mortar from repairing chinks all day in the walls of the outbuildings on the farmstead.

"You two look more like clay statues than real people," said Catherine. "Wash up extra well before eating or you'll be having mud with your food." They planted their hats and soiled coats on the pegs by the door and headed for the kitchen pump.

Next David made his entrance, hanging the tannery keys on another wooden wall peg and covering them with his coat and hat. He turned to secure the door from the brisk dusk breeze, but Samuel's push from outside stopped him. The last of the family had returned to the roost.

Daniel, who had taken his meal at his desk, leaned back against his chair and rolled a blush-red apple, the last of this year's harvest, in his hand. He bit a sizeable gouge from the crisp fruit as he surveyed his children, from one-year-old Nancy to 22-year-old David, at their various stages of eating, or playing or doing their chores.

He coughed soundly for their attention and began, "It appears that we have done well at preparing for wintering-in. *Wiemers mocht so hut mers* - As we make it, so we have it - Not so much left to be done around here that David, Samuel, Elizabeth and Polly can't handle, along with Mama and me. So," he said pointing to each as he named them, "John, Jacob, Susan and Rebecca, this Monday you get yourselves off to school."

John and Jacob's jaws dropped in tandem. At once they began their dual protest. "But Papa, the fences are . . ."

Daniel raised his palm to them and frowned. "When there's time, there's school. A good education will serve you well. You'll see." The boys fell silent and sullen.

Conversely, Rebecca tapped Susan's shoulder and smiled at the thought of spending time at school rather than on household tasks. Susan returned her expression thinking about the chance to see other young folks from the area on a regular basis. Edward Lehman's face, in particular, crossed her mind, though he sometimes upset the schoolmaster with his quick wit that too often amused the other students and disturbed their studies.

Deacon Myers was very strict about his classroom, but Susan didn't mind. His love of learning was obvious because his profession offered a very meager salary that he supplemented by producing beautiful ink and watercolor *Frakturs*, intricately illustrated documents commemorating marriages and births that became treasured family heirlooms. Mama was fiercely fond of the ten brightly-colored *Geburtscheine* marking each of the Royer children's births that were carefully rolled up and stored in Catherine's blanket chest.

"Papa, can I go this year?" begged Cate dashing to his side. "I know my numbers to 100, but I want to read better – like Polly and Elizabeth. Can I, Papa?"

"I think that would be fine, Cate," he said stroking her head. "I keep forgetting how grown up you're getting."

"Oh, thank you, Papa." She pointed up to the far rafter. "And I promise to keep stringing as many beans and apples as Mama wants."

"Yes, Cate has managed quite a collection already," Catherine said. "I think she might be ready for a metal needle for stitching the next time the tinker comes by."

"And I'm anxious for another newspaper," Daniel said. "Now, finish up your duties for the day. It won't be long until the night calls us all to bed."

As the group settled back into their former routine, Daniel fished among the papers on his desk for the well-worn newspaper delivered weeks earlier by the tinker. He spread it out atop his pages of accounts and correspondence and began to re-read the news. Catherine knew it was the business about the British threats of an assault on Washington that he pored over the most. She, too, feared for her children – the family's very way of life, all of their work, might disappear for them and so many others.

Gott in Himmel, she prayed silently. *Keep our family safe. Put peace in those Redcoats' hearts and our lives.* She lifted her youngest from her niche on the floor beside Mukki and hugged her.

"Amen," she whispered.

-17-

Whiling Away the Winter

S arah and Rebecca awoke within seconds of each other and shared sleepy stares without lifting their heads from their pillows. "I can't believe how quiet it is," Rebecca whispered.

"Maybe we packed away our spirits along with Christmas yesterday," Susan said.

The day before the girls had discarded or carefully stored away the family's modest reminders of Christmas. Gone were the small boughs of greenery and window candles. Some German homes followed the unique tradition of displaying a cut evergreen tree decorated with handmade ornaments. Susan envied them as she imagined the scent of pine that would fill the cabin and the shiny punched-tin star on top, a remembrance of the star of Bethlehem. Perhaps Papa would relent one day and they could have one, too. She sighed. The end of any special season was always dreary, but today the silence was unusually intense.

When Rebecca descended the narrow stairs from the loft, the reason for the increased hush was instantly apparent. "Susan, come look! It's the first snowfall."

Snow was still billowing on top of the heavy blanket of white that had accumulated during the night. Peeking out the window, the frantic flurry of snowflakes reminded Rebecca of the time she and her sisters had a pillow fight. It had started as great fun, lots of giggles and squeals, but ended when one of the pillow's seams burst and feathers flew everywhere, followed by a sound scolding. It took them hours to collect all the illusive down.

Susan was soon shoulder-to-shoulder at the window beside her sister. Rebecca tried in vain to follow the fluttering path of a single snowflake to its place on the windowsill. She would choose one high in the air and try to lock her eyes on it until it landed, but against the morning's gray backdrop one snowflake quickly got lost among the others.

"What are you doing, girls?" Catherine called. "Come away from that window or you'll catch a chill. I know the first snow is beautiful, but if you come down *mit die Grippe*, you won't be able to enjoy it."

Rebecca and Susan dutifully scurried to the fireside, but knew that their mother's foremost concern was with the Royer men and hired help who had left the day before to go over the mountain to strip more tanbark for the tannery. Papa had even allowed John and Jacob to go along despite their mother's reservations. When the men had loaded up the wagons with ample foodstuffs and canvas tents for the two-day outing, no one had anticipated the heavy snowfall that now nearly covered the woodpile at the side of the cabin.

Soon Elizabeth, Polly and Cate also gathered beside the warmth of the stove as baby Nan wriggled out of Catherine's arms to play with Mukki's feathery tail. "Well, girls," Catherine said. "There may be no men to care for today, but we still have chores to do before we have a bit of fun ourselves."

Snow continued to fall throughout the day and showed no sign of stopping. Although Daniel and his sons probably had all they needed to endure the sudden storm, they may very well have sought shelter in a farmer's barn or a roadside tavern when it became clear this was no ordinary snowfall. Catherine tried to hide her anxiety, but would not be relieved until they returned safely.

With the men away, cooking and housekeeping duties lightened, but the extra time that only a snowy afternoon could provide fueled Catherine's worries. She and the girls could do little outdoors, although Polly had made the trek to the barn to milk the two cows and returned with warm eggs 'borrowed' from the hens. In the men's absence, the daily routine of preparing massive plates of food was deferred. Catherine and 'her girls,' as she called them, were content with leftover stew and the extra biscuits they had baked yesterday. Susan stitched another letter of the alphabet in her sampler, Elizabeth read scripture from Papa's large leather-bound Bible with its heavy metal hinges and clasp – as Susan would have guessed – and Cate was playing with Jacob's clay marbles, even though he would not be pleased if he knew. She would return them to their leather pouch before bedtime and Jacob would be none the wiser.

In the muffled stillness Rebecca could hear the creak of Mama's rocker, the pull of the rough thread through the linen in Susan's embroidery hoop, the sharp clatter of the marbles and even the soft crinkling of the pages Elizabeth carefully turned. Quiet was quiet, but this was too much quiet for her liking. The walls of the cabin were closing in on her as the early afternoon grayness descended and the snow deepened. She clearly recalled Mama's earlier statement about having some 'fun' of their own and was at the end of her patience waiting for Mama to announce what activity she had in mind.

"Mama," she finally asked, "now that the chores are finished, what can we . . ."

Catherine had wondered which of her girls would be the first to remind her of her earlier promise. She was not at all surprised that it was Rebecca. Before the anxious girl finished, Catherine smiled and said, "You know, today would be a good day for *Scherenschnitte*."

The suggestion met its mark as Rebecca beamed. The other girls had followed the conversation and also caught the fever enough to put aside their tasks and join in the pleasant diversion. Although she wasn't nearly as good at paper cutting as Susan, who excelled at all the domestic arts, Rebecca loved folding the precious squares of paper into triangles, drawing designs and using the sharp sewing scissors to cut delicate patterns that produced a six-sided snowflake all her very own.

The girls watched as their mother pulled out sheets of parchment from her husband's desk along with three tiny pairs of scissors. "Come now, if you put on your shawls you can sit at the table near the window where the light is a little stronger," she said.

Within minutes Rebecca, Susan and Polly were gathered around the table intent on their craft. Parchment was expensive and the girls knew what a privilege it was to have this kind of leisure on such a tiresome afternoon. Elizabeth had considered this undue expense and opted to content herself with the scriptures.

163

Catherine stood back and watched them quietly at work, amazed at how their young hands, so accustomed to the hard tasks of farm work, were able to execute the dainty cuts that resulted in such beautiful symmetry. Catherine recalled that she had been younger than Susan, but older than Rebecca, probably eight years old, when her mother first taught her the Swiss-German art of paper-cutting. Catherine had created dozens of crinkled snowflakes, domestic scenes and valentines in the years before her marriage, some of which still rested between the pages of the large family Bible.

"*Gut, gut.*" Catherine encouraged the girls' efforts as she turned her attention to pickling the eggs that she had hard-boiled earlier that day. She would soak the peeled eggs in dark beet juice that would turn their waxy white flesh a joyful purple. Beet juice and parchment didn't mix and Catherine thought it wise to leave the girls to their happy art. Cate, knowing their mother would never let her come near the sharp scissors, hadn't dared to ask if she could join in, and continued to occupy herself by arranging the amber, azure and citron-colored marbles in a circle on the rag rug in front of the fire.

Tiny snippets of paper covered the table, not unlike the snowflakes that settled on the woodpile outside. From the disapproving furrows on Susan's forehead, Rebecca could tell that her older sister wasn't happy about the erratic shapes

Rebecca was drawing on the outside of the folded paper. Susan preferred perfect circles and squares, not the jagged outlines and irregular shapes Rebecca was making.

"You know, if you held your pencil steady and followed your lines more carefully the cuts would all be straighter," Susan said.

Rebecca refused to be bothered by Susan's pointed suggestion. Her sister was usually supportive, but sometimes a twinge of her carefully guarded competitive nature slipped through. For her part, Rebecca secretly cheered the spindly lines Susan called 'flaws' that set her *Scherenschnitte* apart from the others.

At least I know which paper snowflake is mine, she thought with satisfaction.

While Susan and Rebecca eyed each other's snowflakes warily, they noticed that Polly had immersed herself intensely in purposeful sketching and cutting. She wasn't making a six-sided snowflake. Her *Scherenschnitte* was larger than theirs, and beside her were discarded scraps that she had crumpled, but not enough to disguise that they were heart-shaped.

Then it came to Susan. *Polly isn't making a snowflake, she's making a valentine! Easy to know why*, thought Susan – *George*. Neither she nor Rebecca was old enough to have a special someone who might cherish their finished tokens, but Polly certainly was.

"Wonder who that's for," teased Susan loud enough for Polly but not for their mother to hear.

"Polly's not telling," Rebecca chimed in singsong knowing instantly, as did Susan, that Polly's valentine was for her certain somebody.

Polly ignored them both, intent on her careful cutting. Tiny paper scraps gathered on the table below as she snipped and turned and snipped and turned in rapid precise motions.

Others in the family may not have noticed all the signs of affection Polly had showered on George when she thought no one would notice. And George, though careful not to draw the ire of his taskmaster and Polly's father, was still quick to help Polly haul water buckets from the spring or to join in her search for a missing calf. Susan and Rebecca weren't sure if their mother or Elizabeth noticed or not, but over time Polly and George had stolen every possible moment they could to be together. Then, Susan remembered Polly's bedtime tears weeks earlier – her fears that she and George could never marry – and she chided herself for teasing her sister.

In short order, Polly's intricate circular valentine with eight perfectly rounded hearts encircling an eight-petaled flower emerged. Each of the hearts had a solid middle section surrounded by tiny cutout scrolls and curlicues. Even Susan, who thought herself the most skilled in the craft, was impressed, not only by the speed with which Polly created such a lovely pattern, but by her ability to envision what the finished valentine would look like when she opened the folded packet. Polly smoothed the creation on the table to inspect it. Satisfied, she fetched the inkwell and quill pen from Daniel's desk and continued her work.

"What are you writing?" asked Rebecca watching as Polly etched bits of prose in each of the hearts.

"Just some notes. Nothing much really," said Polly without looking up. Susan noticed that a little tip of Polly's tongue peeked out of the corner of her mouth as it always did when she concentrated on a task that was important to her.

"I wonder when Samuel and Sarah will have their wedding?" Rebecca asked casually, gauging Polly's reaction with a sidelong glance. "You know weddings come in threes. Mrs. Snowberger's daughter just got married to the Harbaugh boy after Christmas, and if Samuel finishes his cabin on schedule, he and Sarah will be ready for the ceremony right after the harvest is in." No one answered her open-ended question.

Polly checked to ensure Mama and Elizabeth weren't watching before holding her circular valentine to the light to re-read her careful script. Catherine was preoccupied with feeding Nan who had awakened hungry from her nap. Elizabeth was still absorbed in her reading.

Rebecca continued her jibe. "Who will be next?"

Susan tried to catch Rebecca's eye to persuade her to ease up a bit.

"You two are as curious as crows," said Polly, preparing to re-fold her completed secret *Scherenschnitte* and tuck it in her pocket.

"Oh, no!" her sisters whispered. "Let us see!"

"It's really none of your concern," Polly said, but she hesitated, resolving that she truly loved George and didn't care if her sisters knew it. Polly felt secure standing beside George. There was no need for her to silently apologize for her sturdy five-foot, nine-inch stature as she did in the company of most other folks. With George she felt safe and pretty and happy – all things good.

"If you feed the chickens for me tomorrow," Polly said with a mischievous gleam, "I'll let you have a look."

It took only a moment for the girls to weigh the task of bundling up against the morning cold and the icy walk to the barn in shoulder-high snow against not knowing what Polly had so carefully inscribed on her valentine. The not knowing was more than they could bear.

"Agreed?" said Polly.

When the two heads nodded, Polly revealed her creation so Susan and Rebecca could see what she had written.

As she silently read the verse, Susan noticed that Polly had made several spelling mistakes, but the meaning of her words was clear. With the lines of her poem centered in each of the valentine's open hearts, Polly's poem read:

As the Rose merry Grows
by thyme
and Grapes Grow round
the vine

So Shure
you are my
Valentine

Oh, may the Heavens
give you grace,

And a smile of Love
Attend your face.

The Rose is read
The vilete Blew

Sugar is
Sweet and so are you

When this you See
Remember mee"

Susan considered pointing out the grammatical errors, but she thought better of it when she saw Polly's delight. Rebecca, who cared even less about correct spelling than Polly, was awed by Polly's ability to both make the valentine *and* composing such a beautiful poem.

"My, my, Polly. When George sees this he will know exactly how you feel about him," said Susan.

"I think he knows already," sighed Polly. "I pray every day that Samuel won't be the only Royer who marries in the fall, but Papa . . ." Her voice trailed off as Susan hugged her and even Rebecca sympathized.

Polly refolded her treasure and slipped it in her pocket. *I just hope I find a way to get it to George before Valentine's Day. Maybe Mrs. Fahnestock will need more help. Dear God, make her candles burn quickly.* Her musings ended when a frantic pounding on the plank door shattered the serenity of the cabin.

"They're here! They're here!" Catherine nearly shouted reacting in shock at the sudden sound and praying it was "her boys."

"Could they be back already?" said Elizabeth who was hopeful but so startled by the interruption that she had nearly let the Bible fall from her lap to the floor.

In seconds Catherine released the latch and opened the door to find Sean McBride, covered in snow, his blue lips trembling and his body shivering. He nearly fell into the room, the panic in his eyes communicating his alarm before he could find the words. "Mama sent me," he wheezed. "Maggie's baby's comin' early, but she's having trouble, awful trouble. Snow's too deep to make it to Doc Bonebreak, so Ma sent me here to fetch you."

"Quick, Polly. Give Sean some hot cider and Susan, get the coverlet from my bed and wrap it around his shoulders," Catherine instructed.

Pulling the ragged, woolen cap from his head, Sean collapsed at the table and greedily sipped the cider, his pale fingers raw with cold.

"Pa and Connor got caught in the blizzard at the White Swan in town and there's no one else to help. Ma's afraid Maggie's gonna die. She's in terrible pain." Panic glistened in his snow-stung eyes.

"Don't worry, Sean. We can help," Catherine assured him. "You warm yourself by the fire while I get some things together."

Susan moved Sean to a stool nearer the stove as Catherine summoned Elizabeth and Polly to her side. "You two need to come with me. I've been worried about Maggie for some time now. She's so young and too small to be carrying a

171

child *and* McBride babies have always been bigger than their mothers can easily bare. I'm going to need all the help I can get. I'll gather my herbs and tonics and you two bundle up fresh linen and clean thread. Put on some extra layers of clothes, too. It's going to be a long, cold walk to the McBrides and I suspect that despite all the trees in the forest, they'll not have enough wood for their fire."

"But what about the younger girls?" asked Elizabeth. "With Papa and the others away, who will look after them?"

Catherine studied the stunned faces of her four youngest. She motioned Susan to her side. "You four young ones have not been left on your own before, but Susan, you're a sharp girl, aren't you?" said Catherine smiling encouragement. Susan's chest swelled at such rare praise. "You are in charge while we're gone."

She then beckoned for Rebecca who was watching them curiously. "Rebecca, you are to be the best of helpers for Susan until we return," she said kissing her cheek. "I'm sure that Cate and Nan will be in very good hands until then." Rebecca looked at Susan to reassure her that she would do her best.

Catherine pulled her woolen cape over her shoulders and gathered up one of the bundles the older girls had readied. "Now hurry," she said to Elizabeth and Polly who were pulling up the hoods of their cloaks and shouldering the rest of the leather bags that carried the supplies Catherine had requested. "We have no time to waste."

Catherine's face wore her solemn 'don't-get-in-my-way' look. Serious business was afoot. Clutching their supplies, the three women and Sean ventured out into the snowy gloom in the direction of the McBride farm. As suddenly as Sean McBride had entered the cabin, they were gone.

With her nose pressed against the window, Rebecca tried to stifle a tear. She didn't want Susan, and especially her younger sisters, to know she was frightened – frightened by the shadowy forms of her mother and sisters disappearing over the ridge – frightened by the thought of a little baby and young mother possibly dying – frightened by being on their own for the first time in their lives. As good German Baptists, they had known since infancy that prayers were for bedtime, mealtimes and Sunday services, but for one of the first times Rebecca could remember, she was praying hard in the middle of the afternoon that the Lord would protect her family – the ones working in the mountains, the ones headed over the ridge and the ones left behind – herself included.

Susan sensed Rebecca's fear and gathered up her courage, resolved to keep everyone in her charge safe. *Busy hands – we need busy hands to calm our hearts*, she quickly determined. "Rebecca, check Nan's diaper and make sure she's wrapped tightly. Cate, fetch some more wood from outside. When you're finished, both of you, we'll gather by the fire and share some scripture and prayers. Bring some mending along. It's going to be a long night and we must all be ready to do our part."

As everyone scurried about, grateful for the chance to act rather than panic, Susan thought, *How can the world handle so much trouble? God keep us all.*

-18-

Neighbors in Need

Catherine smelled the smoke rising from the McBride's leaning chimney even before she saw its white curl fly heavenward in the darkness. It had taken what felt like hours for the three women to plow through the thigh-deep snow. The nearly two-mile trip had wearied them. When they got within earshot of the muffled cries coming from the cabin, they no longer felt the stinging wind in their faces or the heavy weight of the frozen hems of their woolen skirts. Without a word, they trudged toward the ramshackle cabin with renewed resolve.

Fear, blood, and sweat crowded the air inside the poorly lit cabin. Young Maggie writhed in pain on the narrow cot near the fireplace. Mrs. McBride hugged Catherine and each of the girls as they came through the door. With her furrowed brow and disheveled white hair, she was clearly distraught. "Lord be praised! Thank God you've come."

Elizabeth and Polly stood motionless awaiting instructions as Sean slammed the cabin door shut against the wind. As their eyes adjusted to the dim light, the shabby, unclean living area stunned them. Scraps of food from what must have been yesterday's noon meal had congealed to the tin plates on the rough table in the corner and the dirt floor had not been swept in weeks.

Although the girls tried their best not to reveal their shock at the filth and clutter so unlike their own home, the sight momentarily distracted them from the crisis at hand. The only sign of careful tending was the pristine display of porcelain teacups on a shelf nailed high on the wall in the far corner, out of harm's way. When they caught her eye, Polly immediately recalled her mother's recounting of last spring's tea party at this very place. That this cabin was ever the site of so grand a show was inconceivable.

How strange, thought Polly, *that Mrs. McBride is so quick to make uncharitable remarks about others, but cares so little about her own housekeeping. She would do better to barter more for soap than fancy teacups.* But when Polly saw Mrs. McBride so clearly distressed, she quickly abandoned such critical thoughts.

On their approach to the McBride's cabin, Polly had seen that her mother's suspicions were confirmed – very little firewood had been split. That explained the rusty ax resting idly against the tiny woodpile beside the hearth. Daniel Royer had taught all of his children that their lives depended upon how

176

well they maintained the farmstead's tools. Everyone in the family knew to clean and carefully store the implements in their proper places after each use, and, as a family, they reverently oiled the trowels, shovels, rakes, chisels, awls and saws once a year. 'Take good care of your tools and they will take good care of you,' Daniel often said.

On the Royer farmstead, stockpiling wood for the winter was a summer long endeavor. Well before the first autumn winds, they stacked cords of wood in neat rows ready to keep the cooking fires burning and the family warm.

Catherine looked past Mrs. McBride at Maggie's pale face and contorted movements and knew instantly that the young mother-to-be was having difficulty bearing her child. "How long has she been in labor?"

"Nearly a day and a half," said Mrs. McBride. "The pains began just after Silas and Connor started for town. This snow has probably stranded them there."

Catherine hid as best she could her dismay at her neighbor's delay in summoning her.

If only they had sent for me earlier, much earlier, thought Catherine. *Such a lengthy labor strains not only the mother, but the infant as well.* She studied Maggie's sweating brow. *To my mind, John Barley Corn has stranded those men, not Jack Frost.* She raised a silent prayer for guidance to help

Maggie through this crisis and offered another one of gratitude for her own family of sometimes sullen but sober men.

Catherine knelt by the sour smelling bed as she squeezed Maggie's hand and calmly issued orders to all of them. "Polly, you and Sean bring in some more wood and get this fire blazing. Elizabeth, draw some water and set it to boiling. Jane, I will need some clean linens. Tear up some shirts or sheets if you must. We brought some with us, but not nearly enough."

Catherine's use of Mrs. McBride's first name shocked Elizabeth. Longtime neighbors and even the closest of friends rarely called one another by their given names. It confirmed Elizabeth's fear that something about this birth was terribly wrong.

"Now, now Maggie," Catherine murmured in the frightened girl's ear while applying a damp handkerchief to her forehead. "You're going to have your little one very soon now."

Maggie just groaned as her hysteria subsided at the sound of Catherine's soothing voice. Exhausted, Maggie closed her eyes.

As ordered, Polly headed back into the cold with her lantern and Sean in tow. The young man followed easily, eager to escape the confines of a cabin bursting with women and their intimate pain. Chopping wood was not his favorite chore, but he was anxious to relieve some stress and not above impressing

Polly with his ability to split the large chunks of hardwood. "Keep it up, Sean," said Polly adopting her mother's air of authority. "We're going to need all the logs you can manage."

"Don't know what all the fussin's about. Most of the cows just drop their calves in the fields," grumbled Sean. "Don't know why it should be so hard for Maggie."

"People are different than cows, Sean," Polly scolded. "Maggie isn't some field animal and babies are special gifts from God. We need to do everything we can to help out . . . and pray that they will be all right."

By the time Polly and Sean struggled through the door with armloads of wood, Elizabeth was stirring up a tincture of birthwort that had been harvested months before from their four-square garden. Elizabeth touched the liquid with her fingertip to test the temperature, then poured it into a tin cup, stirred it with a small, wooden spoon and handed it to her mother.

Polly shuddered as Maggie swallowed the mixture that Catherine tenderly dripped into her mouth while cradling the young woman's head as tenderly as a child's. Polly could barely go near the smelly, dirty yellow birthwort flowers that bloomed in late fall. Harvesting and grinding the bitter seeds that were part of the concoction that Maggie was now choking down her throat had been really unpleasant. Since childhood, Polly's job was to keep the little ones away from the plant's poisonous flowers and seeds. What irony that a plant so foul, could, in tiny doses, ease a woman's suffering in childbirth. In spite of the relief it offered, she shuddered at the thought of how it must taste.

"Good girl, Maggie," said Catherine urging the last of the liquid into Maggie's puckered mouth. "This will ease the pain. You'll feel better soon."

But as the minutes, disguised as hours, passed, Maggie did not get better. Her moans subsided, but the pain etched in her face did not.

Then Maggie cried out anew as a stabbing pain hit her. As her agony intensified, everyone held captive by the smothering, emotion-packed cabin prayed that the baby would come soon. Catherine was doing the best she could to help usher this new life into the world, but she knew that both souls might be bound for another world. Only God could save them now. Catherine could only be His instrument.

As the time of anxious waiting limped along, Polly rested her head in her hands, thinking that she should soon bring in more firewood. She was turning to the far corner of the cabin to ask Sean to help, when Maggie let out a piercing scream that was quickly followed by the weak cry from a gasping newborn. Polly jumped and held her breath as she turned praying for good news from her mother.

"It's a boy, Maggie," said Catherine as she handed the tiny baby to Mrs. McBride who swaddled the child in a prized tablecloth. Maggie smiled feebly, eyes half-open, but all the color had drained from her face and wet curls were pasted to her forehead.

Catherine continued tending to Maggie, bathed her face and freshened her dressings and bedding. Finally, she took the infant from Mrs. McBride and placed him in his mother's arms.

Over the next hour the cabin became hushed with exhaustion and concern. The girls marveled at the baby's tiny fingers and the soft down on his tender head. They were all relieved that Maggie's cries had ceased and hopeful that the most difficult of her trials was over. But in the flickering firelight, Elizabeth noticed with alarm what Catherine already knew. Her worst fears were emerging as she watched the newborn as he lay limply at Maggie's breast where Catherine had placed him to nurse. Both Maggie and her tiny son were struggling to breathe. The stricken expression on Catherine's ashen face told her and the others that Maggie and her son were dying.

"Shall I share a psalm, Mother?"

"Yes, dear, scripture may give poor Maggie and her son some comfort."

"Dear God, no!" keened Mrs. McBride. "Not both of them. Don't take both of them."

Polly instinctively moved to support the wailing woman who was near collapse. Mrs. McBride fell against her shoulder, the tears streaming down her face.

Elizabeth closed her eyes and began, *"Der Herr ist mein Hirte, Mir wird nichts mangeln . . ."*

"Nein, nein Liebchen, auf English bitte," said Catherine stroking Maggie's forehead.

Elizabeth paused at her mother's gentle reminder that neither Maggie nor her mother-in-law could comprehend her German recitation. She started again . . . "The Lord is my Shepherd, I shall not want . . ."

The sun was rising over the eastern hills as Catherine dragged her way toward home.

I couldn't even anoint them into God's hands as I would have if they were believers, she lamented silently. The small bottle of oil had never left her pocket because she had sensed that, as much as she wished to offer it, the gesture would not have been proper.

She had sent Elizabeth and Polly on ahead while she helped Mrs. McBride as much as she could with the somber task of preparing the bodies for burial. The sorrowful image languished stubbornly in Catherine's mind. Although death had brought with it the end of pain and allowed sweetness to return to Maggie's face as the pale infant, so newly born, so shortly lived, rested in her arms, the pain of the loss overpowered everything. The two looked as if they were simply sleeping, but their cold skin betrayed the false hope.

"So tragic," Catherine whispered shaking her head. She couldn't help but recall her own despair when the Lord had taken three of her infants. "How could someone as young and frail as Maggie, with so little family stability or faith – how could she have endured it? Perhaps that is why the Lord took her, too."

The snowy landscape glistened in the morning sunlight. Admiring the dawn's warm, new glow even after the grimmest of nights, Catherine pondered the mysteries of God's will.

Why should this young woman die with her first child while God has blessed me with ten healthy births? Thoughts turned to her own daughters. Her dear Elizabeth and Polly, so close to marrying age, had witnessed Maggie's agony and seen an infant die within moments of its first breath, barely opening his eyes before they were shut forever. Catherine wished they could have been spared that experience. *Childbirth is frightening enough without such memories. I can only pray that my daughters' health and strength and God's mercies allow them to safely bear strong, hearty children*, she thought. She brushed tears from her eyes as she recalled her own mother's comforting wisdom. "God's ways are not our ways . . . His will be done."

As she reached the oxcart path that separated the Royer farmstead from the McBride's land, she caught the first glimpse of her cabin where she trusted the young ones had gotten safely through the night and where Polly and Elizabeth would be preparing a large breakfast for the men who would soon return home.

She squinted into the bright sun to discern a lone figure approaching through the snow. In a moment, she recognized Daniel. He had returned unharmed from the storm. She could see the worry in his face as he came nearer. "Oh Catherine," he said taking her in his arms. Within his sheltering embrace, she finally allowed herself to weep.

Daniel hugged her to him as she cried, remembering with a stab to his heart how difficult Nan's birth had been. Of all the children Catherine had bore him, that birth was the closest he had come to losing her. Mrs. Snowberger who had helped with that delivery had shooed him out of the cabin, but from outside the window he had heard Catherine's cries. He recalled his fears of losing her and of wondering how he would manage the family without her.

As Catherine's warm tears dampened his wool coat, Daniel prayed silently. *Thank you God for this woman who has shared my life, for the children You have given us, and for this land where we are making a better life for our family.*

"*Gott ist gut,*" Catherine sighed as her sobbing subsided, "isn't He? Even when he takes the young and innocent from us?"

"*Ja, da stimmt. Gott ist immer gut,*" Daniel answered.

He kissed the top of her head. He would wait with her here in the cold until she was ready to continue to the cabin. He would stay with her – always.

"God be praised," he said to himself. "I am so blessed."

-19-

Trouble at the Kiln

Winter was still hanging on in the Cumberland Valley, but its grip was definitely loosening. Morning's light came sooner and twilight lingered past the serving of evening supper. Ice blocks were stored in the barn having been cut from the millpond weeks before when the water was frozen to its maximum thickness. The Lord had been generous with snowfall. Nearly all the Royer children had sledded down the hillside on old shovelheads. Polly and Elizabeth had even persuaded Catherine to take a turn while the dough was rising, and the little ones laughed to see their mother squeal with delight as she careened down the slope.

Despite the daily chores, the boys found time for snowball battles and everyone took turns visiting neighbors in their new horse-drawn sleigh. But folks accustomed to four seasons felt a familiar yearning to thaw their bones in the strengthening sunshine and match the more rapid cadence of spring. The rafters of the Royer mill swelled in the warmer air. For months the grinding stones had been relatively silent,

186

ceasing the incessant grumble that marked the last of the harvest season as the stone wheels turned the grain to flour. Reba and Bessie pawed at the frost-burnt fields searching for the struggling new green shoots that would soon add a subtle richness to their milk. The scratching and cavorting at the chicken house had noticeably increased as their feisty rooster crowed a little earlier each morning. Even Mukki deserted her designated place near the hearth and was now almost constantly underfoot. Life had been stagnant for too long. The quiet had wrung itself out.

On this late-February morning, uncommon whispers of spring were stirring. Nature was flexing its sinews in the faint pulsing of barely perceptible renewed growth. Susan sensed it the second she opened her eyes – the charge in the air. When she spied the iron augers leaning by the door as she made her way to her steaming breakfast mush, the restless anticipation of eventual spring was confirmed.

Papa must have felt the change too, and had determined that the large stand of frozen sugar maples nearly two miles northeast of the house had thawed enough to begin releasing their sweet sap. Daniel and his sons, using corkscrew augers would bore holes through the bark in some 150 tree trunks. Spiles inserted into the bark of the trees would siphon some of the nectar into the keelers suspended from pegs and dangling below the holes. Forty gallons of sap would yield one gallon of syrup after lengthy and carefully monitored boiling in huge iron kettles. Honey from their bee trees, nearly 70 pounds each year, provided most of their needs for sweetening, and even some preserving, but maple syrup was different; distinct, smooth, lusciously delicious. *Just perfect for those special candies for Samuel's wedding*, Susan thought.

As the household awakened, the Royer cabin buzzed with the increased pulse of life. Baby Nan popped up nearly everywhere now that her newfound climbing and crawling skills helped her discover life outside of her cradle. Fortunately, Mukki was an able monitor of the babe, blocking her curious forays toward the hearth and loft stairs and endless other dangers lurking about the household. Cate had perfected her skills at annoying her older brothers by snapping their suspenders or tapping their shoulders and disappearing before they discovered her. Only Papa and David were spared her antics.

Samuel, as usual of late, was out the door before the rest of the family had their morning nourishment, anxious to make headway on his new cabin, but without shirking his normal responsibilities. Stacks of shaved logs and split shingles waited in the barn for the cabin-raising he hoped would happen by April.

The demise of the harshest part of winter had Polly atwitter as she anticipated the tannery workers spending more time at the farmstead rather than off in the distant mountains cutting timber. The natural impulses of teenage boys had John and Jacob constantly poking or arm-wrestling or otherwise accosting each other with the pent-up energy they weren't able to expend with their shorter list of chores. Susan and Rebecca's giggling was starting to drive the rest of the family to distraction.

Only the parents and the eldest had learned how to curb the antics brought on by seasonal change. Daniel, Catherine, David and Elizabeth were doing their best to maintain a modicum of order and decorum in the household but even they, truth be known, were not immune to the stir.

"It is obvious that the extra energy in this house needs to be harnessed," Daniel said as Mukki flew past him to intercept Nan's approach to the slop bucket behind the kitchen pump. "Don't you agree, *mein Frau*?

"*Ja, so,*" said Catherine.

Elizabeth scooped Nan away from the impending mess and added with an urgency she rarely revealed, "Please, Papa, before the walls cave in!"

"Everyone to the table, *schnell*!" he shouted.

In one instant the room was still and silent, and in the next, an anxious scrambling to the table ensued. All eyes focused on Daniel.

"So the temperature takes a bump up and everyone gets *ferhoodled,* huh? We must not squander such enthusiasm, right?" Daniel paused. No one ventured a response. "Right?" he barked.

The children jumped and nodded their heads in unison, "Yes, Papa."

"We are all agreed then. This is what I propose. I have no doubt this warmer air will vanish as suddenly as it has come. In the time we have, let us be productive and make the best of it before it's gone."

Daniel cleared his throat and addressed each in turn.

"Now then, Cate, Elizabeth is your guide today. Whatever she tells you, you must obey. She has much to teach you now that you're becoming a young lady, don't you Elizabeth?"

Elizabeth bounced Nan on her hip and smiled at Cate.

"Maybe it's time you came to know the spinning wheel a little better. We shall see. The weaver will be making his rounds before we know it and there are still piles of flax and wool to be spun."

"Now, what about our Polly?" Daniel asked looking at Catherine. His wife knew he was counting on her to find a safe assignment for this daughter – one as far away from any encounter with George Schmucker as possible. Just two days earlier Daniel had discovered Polly's special handkerchief rumpled among some sweepings at the tannery. Although he had not confronted Polly with the evidence, the stitched initials and heart had spoken for themselves.

"I can make a list of chores as long as my arm. I could surely use Polly as my special helper today,' Catherine said.

"I see no problem with that, do you, Polly?" Daniel assented.

"No, Papa." Polly nodded in Catherine's direction.

"Gut," Catherine said. "We can start with *der Nachekiwwel,*" she added with a wry grin. "The new moon left it so dark last night that not many made their way to the privy." Polly crinkled her nose but dared not object.

Daniel looked next at his eldest. "David, take stock at the tannery. Look for any thawing at the liming pits or mildew in the drying rooms and then inspect the mill for vermin. We'll let Samuel to his cabin preparations today. Tell, him that as you pass the barn on your way to the tannery, son."

David tightened a bit at the mention of the cabin that by rights he, rather than Samuel, should be building for his intended bride. But as he had learned to do, he kept bitter thoughts to himself and simply said, "I'll be on my way now, if

191

that's agreeable, *Vater*." Daniel nodded and David pulled on his coat and hat and was out the door never taking his eyes from the dirt floor.

Jacob elbowed John knowingly at David's response. Jacob tried to ignore it, but the gesture wasn't lost on their father. He cleared his throat again and stared hard at his two younger sons. "And you two boys will be toting a load of buckets and stiles and learning how to auger a maple at just the right spot. I'll make sure you have it right before I make myself busy with the masons at the new house."

"Finally, Susan and Rebecca, with the new house and cabin we'll need much more whitewash than most years. I remember well how much whitewash Mama had me use on this cabin before we were married." Catherine smiled as he continued. "No doubt Sarah Provines will want Samuel to do much the same on theirs. There will be more plants to dust against the bugs as well. So, we need to move plenty of lime from the kiln to the barn. I started a firing last week after the last of the snow had melted."

"I checked the kiln yesterday, Papa," offered Jason. "All the rock and coal were burned down to ash and riddlings and cooled nearly enough for raking out and bagging."

"*Gut*, just as I suspected." Daniel turned back to Susan and Rebecca. "The two of you girls together can manage the handcart, especially with the ground still frozen hard. Mukki can go with you." The spaniel's tail wagged at the hearing of her name. "Take some rakes and shovels from the barn and as you pass the Fahnestock's house on the way to the kiln, pick up some meal bags for the lime. Be careful to keep out the coal ash and riddlings with the gathering. When the thaw is here to stay, everything will be in place to use on the fields with plenty left over for whitewash." Susan and Rebecca warmed at the prospect of being a part of Samuel and Sarah's new life together. Even if the work was hard, it was so romantic.

Susan and Rebecca had chosen the smaller of the two-wheeled, wooden pull carts from the barn; still it was no small burden for them to share. Luckily, the handle, about the size of a broomstick,  was as wide as the four-foot width of the cart's hauling bed, giving them ample room to put their hands behind their backs and hook a hold to pull in tandem, side-by-side. The six-foot depth would give them room to spare for the bags of lime.

They were sweating under their capes when they reached the Fahnestock's front door. The house was situated at the top of a steep embankment above the path to the kiln – quite a climb even without the cart which they had left at the bottom of the hill. Mrs. Fahnestock invited them into the small, limestone structure while her husband fetched the bags they requested from the modest barn behind the house.

"You girls be careful opening the kiln," cautioned Mr. Fahnestock as his wife handed the girls the coarsely woven bags.

"Oh, we've helped John and Polly to gather the lime many times. *Danke*, Herr Fahnestock," said Susan.

"Here are a couple of johnnycakes Andrew didn't eat at breakfast this morning. He was in such a hurry to go hunting. Said this warm air would have lots of creatures stirring.'"

Mrs. Fahnestock handed each girl a warm cornmeal pancake folded into quarters. "You'll need lots of fuel to get the job done today."

"*Danke!*" Both girls smiled as they draped the bags over their arms to accept the treats.

"Amos could come help you, you know," the kindly lady said.

"We'll be fine, really, Frau Fahnestock. Herr Fahnestock needn't bother himself. Besides, Papa sent Mukki along with us. She's waiting just outside."

"It wouldn't be a bother, but I won't insist if you're sure. But, you be careful now."

"Oh, we will, Frau Fahnestock. We promise," Rebecca assured her.

The girls disappeared on the path toward their destination pulling the rattling handcart behind them toward the kiln with Mukki trotting just a few feet ahead. Mrs. Fahnestock watched them shaking her head. "You know, Amos, that Daniel Royer expects an awful lot from his children, if you ask me."

"Well, he didn't ask you, so it's none of our business," Mr. Fahnestock said. "I know what you're saying, but we have to let it alone. Now I'm off to repair that leak in the barn roof."

"The good Lord knows I have plenty to do, too. Annie was up half the night with her coughing. I'll try to get some catnip tonic into her before she nurses the next time," his wife sighed.

"It would probably be Polly with you today instead of me if Mama hadn't asked for her to stay and help at home," Rebecca said to Susan pulling beside her. "Better her than me cleaning the chamber pots." She laughed.

"I think Mama is wise to the sparks between Polly and George and with the tannery workers being more out and about today, she wants to keep a close eye on the two of them. I'm not sure how Papa would feel about George courting Polly, but I like George. He's quiet, but that just gives Polly more room for all of her chatter. They seem like a good match to me," Susan said.

"Me, too. And I think all the marriage fixin's for Samuel and Sarah have Polly more anxious than ever to be courted herself." Rebecca and Susan grinned.

"We may need even more whitewash than Papa thinks," Susan said as the kiln came into sight. Mukki was already waiting for them beside the lower door to the hillside structure.

The second bag of lime ash was nearly at the limit of what they could lift by the time they had cleared the kiln. Their huffing and puffing joined the chorus with Mukki yipping as she chased sounds and shadows, and with the nearby stream burbling under a fine sheet of ice. After heaving the sack into the back of the cart where it rested in a cloud of white dust, the girls paused with their hands on their hips getting their breath. They rubbed their cold, bare hands together. It had been easier to manage the rakes and shovels without their slippery woolen mittens. The lime ash had started to coat the nubby fabric with a thin, chalky slime.

"Oh, look over there," said Rebecca pointing at the ground beside the outside wall of the kiln. "A Snowdrop!" Hugging the stone edge just next to the opening to the grates was a cluster of tiny white blossoms.

"The heat of the firing must have given them a boost to bloom even earlier than usual. I've seen them push up and blossom through the snow some years," Susan said.

As Rebecca crouched to examine the delicate petals, a gust of air blew the hem of her skirt toward the open kiln door. Hidden under the discarded ash below the grates, an almost extinct ember glowed to life. Quickly it fed on the only available fuel, the linsey-woolsey of Rebecca's dress.

Susan gasped as she saw a ribbon of smoke and a sprinkling of sparks float into the air behind her little sister. "Rebecca! Get away from the kiln! You're on fire!" As Rebecca leaped up, Susan lunged toward her to get her out of danger. They collided and tumbled toward the creek.

As they fell, Susan grabbed Rebecca with one hand and with the other reached for the side of the cart to stop their descent down the creek bank. But the cart was resting on uneven ground and it tipped over with the weight of the falling girls. The heavy bags of lime shifted and flipped the cart over directly on top of Susan's extended arm. She howled with pain, but somehow still managed to hold onto Rebecca.

Through her agony she heard Rebecca's screams intensify. The tumble had landed her squarely on the thin surface of the creek and her right leg had cracked the ice. The current, swift with rushing snowmelt from upstream, began drawing her into the opening. It was impossible for her to get a handhold on the smooth, slick ice. Her only lifeline was Susan as they struggled to stay clamped to each others' wrists.

"Susan!" Rebecca wailed floundering like a flag in a gale force wind. "Don't let go of me! Susan!"

Susan had planted her feet squarely against some large rocks on the creek bank that luckily for them were dry from the sun. She secured her grasp on Rebecca's wrist and lay back against the bank pulling with all her might, but Rebecca's anguished flailing in the frigid water flowing beneath the ice threatened to break their grip on each other.

"I've got you. I won't let go!" Susan yelled. Rebecca's panic went on unchecked. "Stop shaking! Stay calm, Rebecca! Just hold on and try to be still. I won't let go. I promise!"

The howls melted into sobs as Rebecca's muscles slackened – all but her hold on Susan's wrist. "Susan," she sobbed. "Pull me out. I'm so cold. I can't get out."

Susan tugged as hard as she could, but the effort triggered the pain in her other arm. She turned and gasped at the curious sight of her forearm, still pinned by the upturned cart. Blood was seeping through her sleeve and the impact of the cart had given the bone of her arm an unnatural bend. She fought the wave of nausea that rose from her stomach. The arm was useless in any attempt to move either herself or her sister trapped in the ice. "I'm trying, Rebecca," she shouted, tears of frustration welling in her eyes, "but I'm not strong enough."

Susan resisted her own fear that her other arm was broken. *If Rebecca panics, I'll lose her*, she thought. "Hang on. I won't let go," she continued to urge.

In the next instant Mukki flew to their side in a frenzy of barking. She snarled at the cart as if to intimidate it into releasing Susan. Having no success, the spaniel floundered down the bank toward Rebecca and slid on the ice and nearly fell into the hole that already held Rebecca captive.

"No, Mukki!" Susan snapped. The dog scrambled to the safety of the bank. "Come here. Come here, girl."

Mukki went to Susan and began licking the tears from her cheeks with her warm tongue. "*Gut*, Mukki," she whimpered. "*Gut* girl."

Rebecca laid her head on her arm, already exhausted, and gave into the power of the freezing water.

Susan's mind raced. *What can I do? What?*

The wind kicked up stinging her cheeks as the winter cold began its untimely return. We could call for help, but the wind will carry our cries the wrong way. She considered the spaniel. *I can send Mukki for help, but how will anyone know what she wants?* She had no hand free to give Mukki anything to carry back as a sign that they needed help. Rebecca's free hand was over the thin ice, out of Mukki's reach. Susan dared not move her feet and risk her hold on the bank. The only thing she was able to move was her head.

"My cap!" she blurted.

"What?" Rebecca stammered from below. "What did you say, Susan?"

"I said 'my cap.' I'll send Mukki back home with my cap." The hood of her cape had already fallen back onto her shoulders. Susan scraped the juncture of her small, white cap and her head against the coarse grass. She felt her hair pull as the cap resisted again and again until it finally fell off. Pushing it with her forehead toward Mukki who lay helplessly panting beside her, Susan puffed, "Here, Mukki. Here, girl." The dog came closer and sniffed the cap. "Take it, Mukki. Take the cap."

The dog looked at her quizzically.

Mukki tipped her head toward the cap quivering in the gusty drafts. "The cap, Mukki. Take the cap home."

At the word 'home,' Mukki's ears perked and she turned and started in the direction they had come.

"Stop, Mukki!" Susan screamed. "Stop!"

"What? What happened?" Rebecca pleaded from the creek. Susan had to ignore her – had to stay focused on her mission.

At Susan's command, and sensing that the girls weren't following, Mukki came running back. Susan sighed in relief.

The wind still shook the cap on the ground between them. Again Susan nodded at it and urged, "The cap, Mukki. Take the cap."

This time the dog complied and took it in her mouth.

"*Gut*! *Gut*, Mukki. Now, go home, girl. Take the cap home, Mukki."

Mukki hesitated.

"Home!" Susan repeated. The dog, now confident in her job, took off with the long white ribbon bands whipping back against her neck.

Susan watched her disappear and prayed, *Mein Gott in Himmel, help her find the way. Help them understand. Please, Lord. Please.*

"Susan?" Rebecca begged for a response.

"I'm right here, Rebecca. Mukki is taking my cap home. They'll come – you'll see. They'll come . . . they have to come"

"But I'm so cold and my arm hurts. I can't feel my feet at all, Susan." She began to whimper. "I'm scared. What if I can't hold on long enough? Until they come."

"Then I'll hold on for both of us. Now, close your eyes and we'll pray. Pray God will keep us safe until then."

-20-

George Saves the Day

George stooped beside the liming pit at the tannery staring at the wood and clay-packed lining. Despite the hard winter, he had found only minimal damage to the clay, merely a few cracks to be patched, and the wood had fared very well even with the bitter temperatures. Most probably the worst of the freeze and thaw cycles were past for the year, so any further problems would be minor.

George always did his best to anticipate problems before they happened. Just last spring he had suggested a second dam be built further upstream from the tannery to avoid flooding because of changes in the creek's drainage caused by expanding growth north of the Royer's land. Had Daniel not heeded George's advice, the operation might have suffered considerable damage with the rising water.

Even so, Daniel and David considered him as nothing more than hired muscle to be paid a fair wage for his sweat. Although they would readily acknowledge that George was

202

smarter than most, it would take more than that to make him a suitable match for one of the Royer daughters.

George made a mental note of the needed repairs. *I'll report this to David up in the drying room*, he thought as he pulled his collar up against the increasingly strong, cold breeze, *but I hope I won't be the one here to fix it. If Uncle Cyrus decides to apprentice me, just about one year from this very day, I'll be able to hire myself out as a full-fledged carpenter, one who can provide for a wife and family.*

He reached into his pocket – the one that had held Polly's handkerchief until two days ago. He dearly missed it and prayed he would find it before any of Polly's family did. They mustn't suspect his intentions until he could live up to them.

George stood and stretched his hefty frame to its full six-foot, one-inch height and gazed up toward the Royer's cabin. Lost in his thoughts of Polly, he barely saved his hat as a gust of wind caught the wide brim and pulled it away from his thick head of hair.

As Mukki raced toward home, she searched the area for someone – anyone. She knew instinctively that the girls were in trouble and that Susan had ordered her to take the cap and go home. She would do exactly what Susan had told her as fast as her legs would carry her.

George had just started toward the tannery when his movement caught the dog's eye. She made a quick right turn and skittered across the frozen creek to intercept him. If she barked, she would drop the precious cap, so her silent, sudden arrival startled George. She shuffled around madly in front of him with the ribbons of the cap jiggling from her teeth.

"Mukki!" said George spying something white in her mouth. The dog was frantic, running toward George, then away, then back again.

"What is it, girl?" He bent down to calm her. "What's that in your mouth?" he asked snagging the suspended ribbons.

At the touch, Mukki dropped her parcel. George recognized what it was and was instantly alarmed. No German Baptist girl he knew would willingly remove her cap. Something was wrong.

"Where did you get this, Mukki?"

The dog took off in the direction of the trapped girls, and then pivoted to see if George was following.

George studied the cap and said to the anxious spaniel. "One of the girls must be in trouble, right girl?" The dog barked again urging George to come.

George's mind and heart raced. *Daniel has the boys off tapping the maples. If I go for David or Samuel – anyone – Mukki might not wait.*

Stuffing the cap into his coat he yelled, "Let's go, Mukki. I'm coming!"

With the frozen ground crunching under his boots George could barely keep up with the dog. Fortunately the wind was at his back helping push him up the rise.

All was quiet outside of the Fahnestock's house as they sprinted past. George paused only long enough to see if he could enlist some help, but found no one readily available to grab for support with whatever awaited him ahead. He considered the imposing rise to the house and calculated that he couldn't afford the time and effort it would take to climb up and search further for someone.

Even so, when he returned to the chase, he realized he had lost sight of Mukki. He hesitated as new panic hit him. *Where did she go?* He scanned the area desperately for some sign of her, when he heard the faint barking ahead. He rushed toward the dog's summons that was soon accompanied by a faint, but frantic voice. "Help! Help! Over here, at the kiln."

The overturned cart was below the level of the kiln and partially hidden by it. The creek was even farther downhill.

George nearly passed by in his alarmed confusion, but Mukki cut him off and led him back. As he approached the kiln, he first saw Rebecca sprawled across the ice and then followed the line of her arm up to Susan who had been hidden by the cart that trapped her arm.

Seeing Mukki, Rebecca looked up and caught sight of George looming over and above Susan. "George! We're down here. Susan, it's George. He's come. Praise God, he's come." Susan struggled to open her eyes.

Mukki circled in front of Susan to the edge of the ice and George followed sidestepping down the bank being careful not to disturb the precarious balance that held the girls. Mukki began licking Susan's tears of pain and relief.

"*Gut* girl, Mukki. You saved us," she whimpered. She and George looked at each other. Her expression was blank, her face the color of frozen ash, her eyes flat and stark. "Oh, George. Thank the Lord you're here. I don't think I can hold her much longer."

George secured a foothold and got a firm grip on Rebecca's arm. "You can let go, Susan. I have her." Susan's hand remained clamped on her sister's arm. George repeated more deliberately to Susan. "It's all right, Susan. Rebecca will be fine. You can let go now."

Susan stared numbly at him. Then she released her hold and collapsed.

George dragged Rebecca as gently as he could from the frozen creek. As soon as she was close enough, she draped her other arm over his shoulder and he gathered her into his arms. She folded into herself and began shivering furiously. "It's all right now, Rebecca." She felt like ice, even through his coat sleeves. "I'm going to lay you down, just for a minute, so I can wrap you up better." He crouched beside her on the ground next to the kiln to shield her from the wind, tore off his woolen coat and swaddled her.

"S-S-S-Susan," Rebecca shivered. "Where's S-Susan?"

"I'm going to get her next. Now stay still, Rebecca. I'll be right back." She burrowed against the stone structure.

George sped back to the creek side and gingerly lifted the cart from the bank. The bags of lime slid to the ground and he propped the cart securely against the back of the kiln.

By the time he got to Susan, she was unconscious. Only the tiny puffs from her blue lips in the frigid air betrayed that she was still breathing. A single glance at the unnatural angle of her arm told George it was broken. He hated to move it, but he couldn't leave her there. At least the bleeding was minimal. Other than the red splotches on her sleeve, there was no pool of blood to indicate she might bleed to death. He could afford to slow his pace enough to take the greatest care in lifting her. As he slid his palms under the injured limb and repositioned it more securely across her chest, he winced at her sharp cry of pain.

He looked at the bags of lime beside them. He very carefully laid her down just long enough to grab the largest one and planted it lengthwise against the inside edge of the cart bed. Then, he scooped Susan up and gently placed her into the cart feet first, securing her folded legs against the back of the cart bed and then propping the shoulder of her injured arm against the bag. Picking up the smaller bag, he wedged it against her other shoulder and side to steady her. She began to tremble like Rebecca, but he had nothing left to cover her.

He looked at Mukki who had been keeping close watch. "Up, Mukki," he ordered pointing to the cart. The dog bounded into the cart and nuzzled against Susan in the limited room still available. Perhaps the dog's warmth would ease some of her quivering.

George gathered the abandoned mittens from the ground. With the greatest of care, he pulled one pair onto Susan's stiff, cold hands. He moved the cart away from the kiln and onto the makeshift path beside the creek, the very path that the girls had followed earlier. Each unavoidable bump made him cringe in sympathy with the jostling to Susan's broken body.

Rebecca was still huddled in his coat beside the kiln where he had left her. She was freezing, but otherwise, as far as George could determine, unhurt. He moved to her side to rouse her.

"Rebecca," he urged. "Rebecca," he repeated a bit louder. She lifted her eyes to his. "I have Susan in the back of the cart," he explained. "Her arm is broken and she's unconscious. Can you hear me? Do you understand?"

Rebecca nodded. "*Ist gut.*"

"Now listen closely," he said. "There's no more room in the cart. If I lift you onto my back, do you think you can wrap your arms around my neck and hold on until we get back to the cabin?"

"I'll try," she murmured.

George smiled. "A strong girl like you? I know you can do it. Now, sit up." He held her shoulders and helped her to sit up and lean her back against the kiln. Then he knelt down in front of her, his back facing her. "Now, slip your hands under my suspenders and wrap them around my neck."

She labored to do exactly as he requested.

"*Wunderbar*, Rebecca" he encouraged. He loosened the fastener on the top of his trousers. "Now, wrap your feet around my waist and tuck them into my waistband. I have to pull the cart, so my pants will hold you instead of my arms. Understand?"

"Yes, George." She burrowed her cold, wet feet as he had asked. The Antietam's swift current had stolen both of her boots.

"Just right. Great job, Rebecca. Hold on tight. I'm going to get up now." As he leveraged himself forward and upward, he prayed silently, *Dear Lord, make these suspenders strong. Let them hold until we're safe.* He leaned forward from the waist as far as he could to lessen the strain on Rebecca's arms. Backing up to the cart, he hooked his hands around the pull bar.

George breathed deeply to clear his mind. With the weight of the load and Susan's condition, George reasoned that going to the Fahnestocks, though closer than the Royers, was not the best course of action. *First, I'll have to leave the girls in a very vulnerable position, if only for a few minutes, to scale up the hill to the Fahnestock's door. Then, if Mrs. Fahnestock is the only one home, she can do little to help. Finally, the Fahnestock's have only their plow mule, a slow ride into town for the doctor.*

As it was, the girls were stable, at least for the moment. *Better,* he decided, *to stay with the girls and take the flattest, shortest path to the Royers.*

George searched the northeast horizon; the log house was a clearly visible beacon nestled below the barn. He paused to get his bearings. *I remember seeing Daniel head off north with the younger boys, but David and Samuel should be nearby and Tillie would make good time fetching Dr. Bonebreak. The house is just a little over a half mile from here. God willing, I can get them there quickly.*

Confident in his decision, George secured his grasp on the cart and lowered his head against the elements to begin the journey. *Dr. Bonebreak*, George thought as he pushed his pace to the limit. *I never realized how appropriate that name could be for a doctor – until now. Pray God he can unbreak poor Susan's arm.*

The headwind bent the brim of his hat down across his forehead partially blocking his view. The wind resistance increased his burden, but would help him maintain the slower pace that would lessen the jostling to his injured passenger. *What happened to this morning's warm breezes?* thought George. The powerful gusts checked his natural impulse to run with all possible speed to shelter. If he wasn't careful, he could do more damage getting Susan to safety.

"Hang on, Rebecca. We'll be home soon. Just close your eyes and whisper a prayer for Susan." He felt her arms tighten slightly around his neck in response as he hazarded the continuing steps of the journey.

Polly made her way down the stairs from the boys' loft with the third of the cabin's chamber pots in the crook of her arm. The other two, one from the girls' loft and the other from her parents' sleeping alcove off the kitchen, waited by the front door. As she juggled the three smelly containers and backed out the open door toward the outdoor privy, she found it difficult to remind herself that some chores could be even more unpleasant than this one. She welcomed the return of the winter wind as it blew the fumes of the pots south and she could turn her head north and breathe cleaner air.

She was about to step from the porch when she caught sight of the cart moving toward the house from the direction of the kiln. *Oh, the girls are finally home. Just in time to help peel the potatoes for noon meal*, she thought.

But something didn't look right. Polly squinted to get a better focus and identified one figure, not two, pulling the handcart. As she watched it draw nearer, she recognized the tall, hunched figure. "It's George!" she exclaimed. She quickly stacked the pots against the side of the cabin and hurried toward him. *What does he have on his back?* she asked herself. *And where are Susan and Rebecca?*

Her questions were soon answered.

George raised his head at her approach. "Praise God. We made it. Do you hear, Rebecca? We're home!"

Polly met them, her eyes wide with fear. She laid one

212

hand on George's shoulder and stroked Rebecca's head with the other while she gazed at Susan and Mukki in the cart. "Oh, George – Rebecca, what happened?" George kept his steps steady with Polly now keeping pace.

"George saved us," Rebecca whimpered before George could answer. "But Susan's hurt. Her arm's broken and . . . and . . ." She hugged George and began to cry.

"Mama! Mama!" Polly yelled running ahead.

Cate got to the door before her mother.

"Cate!" Polly shouted. "Susan's hurt. Go to the barn and fetch Samuel. Tell him to come quickly and bring Tillie with him. Run, Cate. Run!"

Even Cate sensed the urgency and sped away without delay. Catherine was right behind her making a beeline for George and the girls.

"Dear Lord. What's happened?" she pleaded. Without waiting for a response, she assessed the situation. "Polly, take Rebecca off of George's back." George paused bending his knees while Polly gathered Rebecca into her arms.

Samuel came running from the barn, leading Tillie behind him. Catherine spied Cate beside the horse. "Cate, go fetch David from the tannery," she ordered.

Elizabeth stood at the door holding Nan. "Elizabeth, get some blankets and make my bed ready for Susan . . . and stoke up the fire. Hurry!"

Samuel tied the horse to the porch post and relieved George of the weight of the cart. "I've got it, George," Samuel offered, his voice full of gratitude. George turned his stiffly drawn face to Samuel as he loosened his hands. "Go inside and get warm, George. I'll take her now. You go rest."

Although George ached with exhaustion, he was hesitant to surrender the girls, even to their family. Safe shelter was too close now – he would leave nothing to doubt.

He advised the others, "Her arm's broken pretty badly. Be careful when you move her. Be really careful." Polly lead him through the cabin door as she carried Rebecca. George collapsed on a stool just inside as she rushed her sister to the warmth of the hearth and started to remove the shivering girl's wet stockings.

Samuel rested the handle of the cart on the raised edge of the wooden porch. Catherine stood beside the cart stroking Susan's forehead and looked at the dog still nestled beside her. "*Gut* girl, Mukki. Go inside now." The spaniel hesitated. "Inside," Catherine repeated gently. As the dog complied, David approached from the tannery. Surveying the scene, he looked to Samuel for an explanation.

"We need to get Susan inside," Samuel said. "Take care – her arm is broken. George Schmucker just brought her and Rebecca back from the kiln. We don't know what happened yet. I'm going to fetch Dr. Bonebreak.

"The augers were going into the bark pretty easily until this blasted wind picked up," Daniel growled. "As soon as we set the spiles in the holes we've already drilled, we might as well get on back home and find something more productive to do."

John was straining to turn the bit of the auger further into the large sugar maple. Beads of sweat sprouted along his eyebrows. "Should I keep trying with this one, Papa?" he asked.

Daniel came over to inspect the work. "Barely made a dent, son. Give it up for now and help Jacob with the stiles and double-check that the keelers are secure underneath. When that's done, gather what we haven't used and we'll head home." He marked the progress of the sun, now partially blocked by flat, gray clouds.

"With the wind at our backs, we'll be home well ahead of supper. Just a bit over a mile to go."

As Daniel and the boys crossed over the footbridge just above the tannery, Daniel pointed to the barn. "Store those things where we can get to them easily next time the weather breaks." John and Jacob broke away in the direction of the barn as Daniel continued toward the cabin.

He scanned the immediate area for signs of activity and spied the handcart propped on the porch and frowned. *Looks like at least one job isn't finished yet. What were those foolish girls thinking, leaving that out in the weather?*

When he stepped on the porch and saw the abandoned sacks of lime, his anger cranked up another notch. He pushed the front door open in fury ready to deliver a harsh rebuke to the girls. Before he could speak, he saw Polly at the table sitting entirely too close to George Schmucker and holding his hand. Between the abandoned handcart and the unseemly handholding, Daniel flew into a rage. "Polly! George! Just what do you think you're doing?"

George stared silently into Daniel's wild eyes. He then tipped his head toward the hearth where Rebecca huddled next to Elizabeth. Daniel reluctantly paused his tirade to follow George's lead. When his gaze settled on the pathetic sight, he rushed to their side. As he took Rebecca into his arms, Elizabeth silently nodded behind them to Susan on the bed with Catherine kneeling beside her.

Daniel gazed at his wife. "*Mein Gott!* What happened to our girls?"

Catherine held a rag drenched with whiskey on Susan's forearm. Elizabeth went to the table and began grinding poppy seeds with the mortar and pestle to add to the milk warming by the fire. The mixture would sedate Susan if she regained consciousness before the doctor, pray God, arrived. Rebecca clung to her father as he crossed over to Catherine and laid his trembling hand on her shoulder.

Catherine placed her hand on top of Daniel's. "Ask George, if he has strength left to tell you. Bless him, were it not for him, the girls . . . the girls . . . " She stopped speaking lest she break down – and she had to stay strong – she had to.

Daniel squeezed his wife's hand. He moved to the table, took off his hat, and sat down across from George. Polly had shifted on the bench they shared to a respectable distance. With a gentle look, Daniel dismissed her. Catching his message she stood. "Let me get both of you some warm cider."

"*Danke*," both men answered.

George watched her move to the shelves where the tankards stood until Daniel's commanding gaze silently bid him begin. "Earlier today I was out by the tannery pit when Mukki came running over carrying this." He picked up the soiled white cap lying on the table. "I followed her to . . ."

Dr. Bonebreak had come, set Susan's arm, and gone. Many long hours later Susan had finally drifted into a peaceful sleep on a temporary sleeping pallet just a few feet away from her parents' bed. Everyone was abed.

The angst that had overtaken the household eased into the quiet rhythm of relief and the cozy hearth was set to burn down to the morning embers just hours away. Catherine and Daniel had given prayerful thanks together with their children and then lay at peace in their alcove. Both were aware of each other's wakeful breathing, but cherished the silence.

Unbeknownst to Catherine, Daniel had been turning Polly's lost handkerchief, still soiled and creased, over in his hands. Just before giving himself over to sleep, Daniel spoke. "Catherine, I think that I was over anxious and premature about tapping the maples today." He handed her the handkerchief. "I believe I have also been premature in my feelings toward George Schmucker. *Er ist ein guttes Mann.*"

"Yes," Catherine agreed, "a very good man indeed."

In the girls' loft, Polly had moved to Susan's bed to comfort Rebecca, whose limbs were still chilled even with the extra bed warmer Mama had prepared. Just before drifting off to sleep, Rebecca wiggled a bit in her sister's arms and asked, "Is it all right if I love George, too."

Polly smiled and made no attempt to deny her feelings any longer. "Yes, Rebecca. He is a good man to love. Now, go to sleep, *Leibchen.*"

-21-

A Day at the Fair

It's all your fault," Susan complained. "It's the first town fair of the spring and I can't go – all because of you." She glared at her splinted left arm, the wooden restraints and tight linen wrappings, her constant companion for more than month. Pouting at the rushing water of the creek, she picked up a nearby stone with her free hand and threw it into the current with such fury that she nearly lost her balance.

After she managed to steady herself she thought, *Whew! Good thing I didn't fall down and hurt myself all over again.* She lowered herself to a patch of new grass warmed by the sun streaming through the barely-budding branches of the towering oaks above the creek bank. Escape from a near tumble and the beauty of the pastel blossoms around her lifted her spirits. She pulled a few tender shoots of grass and sprinkled them on the leather straps that bound the wooden slats and wool padding to her mending arm.

"At least I don't have to work the butter churn or spread manure on the four-square garden, thanks to you. I can't be angry about that," she shared with her bandaged sidekick. Like most friends, the relationship was both frustrating and rewarding. "And there will be more town fairs – the season has just begun."

A robin lit barely six feet away from her and proceeded to peck at the softened ground. *Another sign of spring*, she thought with a smile. *My first robin red-breast.* The bird's arrival prompted memories of a similar encounter close to where she now sat, but a year earlier. *My, such a lot has happened since then*, she mused.

Behind her, the nearly-completed, new stone house cast a tall shadow toward the barn. The anticipated move from their faithful log home would happen just after the arduous planting chores were completed – a matter of weeks. Last year this time, their new home was not even under roof; now the whitewash was flying onto the walls.

"Whitewash," she said. The recent sequence of events ran through her mind – the need for lots of 'whitewash,' the trip to the kiln, the accident, George's rescuing her and Rebecca, Papa's new acceptance of George, the probability of his engagement to Polly – so many things.

She ran her fingers along the grass-strewn leather of her splint. "I guess that good news is 'all your fault,' too," she said recalling her recent negative accusations. "Actually, I'd rather think that it's the fault of the Lord," she considered more reverently. "He works in mysterious ways, His will to be done," she recited to the robin who then took flight.

"Daydreaming again, I see," laughed Samuel making his way from the barn, past Susan, toward the gristmill to begin the spring maintenance. "Leaving all of the chores to the rest of us, huh?"

A stab of guilt returned Susan to the present. "I do what I can," she said. "Mama is always telling me to be careful so that my arm heals right and strong."

"So you can help when the real spring work begins, I'll wager," Samuel teased, but he sensed her frustration. "If you help me count grain bags and chase out the mice at the mill, I'll have more time to check on the grinding stones and gears," he said.

"I'm sure Mama wouldn't mind me doing that," she said following him. "I just need to be back to the house in time to help however I can with the noon meal."

"Fine," Samuel said. "Things are moving quickly here today. Everyone's excited about going to the fair."

"I know," she sighed, slowing her step.

Catching her mournful tone, he immediately regretted what he had said, forgetting the possibility that she might have to remain at home. He waited for her to catch up and put his arm around her.

"But more fairs will come, although I've heard that some folks are upset by how disorderly they're becoming. It's more important that you're in good shape to help at my cabin-raising. Papa is anxious to get back the room in the barn that's filled with my new beams and rafters and such. I'm hoping it can happen before the family moves to the big, new house. "

His reference had the desired effect. "I wouldn't miss the cabin-raising for anything," she said.

"And maybe," Samuel added, "I'll even be able to host a small barn-raising before the wedding in early November, the good Lord willing."

The pace of work was more harried than usual this early spring morning as everyone doubled their efforts to allow them the reward of going to the festivities in Waynesburg later that day. Spring was too new for fresh produce stands, but early flowers, fresh baked goods, games and reconnecting with neighbors unseen for the long winter months would create an exciting atmosphere in the small town. A fair amount of business would be done with the local taverns that always resulted in some inebriated folk roaming the streets, but not enough to spoil the day.

All of the Royers were going, except for the injured Susan and Elizabeth who had readily offered to stay at the farmstead to keep Susan company and to watch over Nan. She knew that would allow her mother, Catherine, the opportunity to enjoy the fair without the constant monitoring of the rambunctious 18-month-old girl. Even the tannery workers and other hired help would be granted a half day off to join the celebration.

While Elizabeth lingered over her needlework keeping an open ear for Nan who was at her afternoon nap, Susan roamed in the clean, fresh air outside her home of nearly ten years. She brushed the rough ground with a fallen oak branch still festooned with last autumn's dried leaves that she had found along the stream. Unlike the foliage of other hardwoods that flushed with bright hues and dropped quickly to the ground, the curled, brown leaves of the oak held onto the limb tenaciously, often not giving up until new buds pushed them off the following spring.

The last of the horses and wagons had disappeared with the rest of the family up the road to Waynesburg hours ago. The absence of the familiar sounds that left with the group amplified those noises that remained – the scratch of her *broom*, the hush of the breeze, the gurgling of the stream, bird choruses, neighing horses and grunting pigs feasting on noon meal leftovers.

She glanced at the western horizon and imagined the impending birth of a new household. But in spite of the thrill she felt about Samuel's marriage to Sarah, this quiet afternoon introduced a sad note.

I'll miss him, she pondered. *Who will calm Papa and David besides Mama? Who will give Rebecca and me horsey back rides? John and Jacob are getting bigger, but they're not strong enough yet. I know Samuel will be happy with Sarah – and he absolutely deserves to be happy. I wouldn't change that, but . . . but . . .*

"I don't think I'm ready yet," she whispered. She studied the oak leaves on the branch in her hand and felt some sympathy for their reluctance to let go.

As she drew near the gray fieldstone wall of the new house, she could see the edge of their tiny log home just behind it. The eerie silence of the deserted new building made it suddenly cold, unwelcoming. Looking at the upstairs window of her long-awaited new bedroom, she rubbed the small of her back and imagined Cate snuggling against her at night. *I'll miss that, too, when she moves to her own bed.* A tear rolled down her cheek.

She wiped it away as she yelled at a squirrel that scurried past her and into the juniper tree that she and her older sister had planted in the new front yard, "And that George Schmucker can hardly wait to take Polly away, too." She plopped to the ground, angry at the world.

"Tillie is chomping at the bit. The warm spell has her wanting to cut loose," said David to Samuel as they rocked in their saddles holding the family horses to a steady walking gait as they made their way home after a long afternoon at the Waynesburg fair. The elder brother tightened up his reins as the horse tossed her head in protest. "It's a little over a mile to the footbridge at the tannery. Think Elsie can keep up if we give them their heads?"

"She'll do better than keep up. The way she's prancing today, I'll wager that Tillie will be eating her dust before we get there," Samuel countered.

"Oh, yeah? Let's go then," David said. Both brothers secured their hats as they leaned low and forward in their saddles. They loosened their reins and poised themselves for action. "On three. *Eins – Zwei – Drei!*" When the men kicked the horses' flanks giving them leave to their enlivened spirits, the beasts broke into a lively gallop.

The pounding of hooves suddenly drew Susan's attention away from the cluster of dried oak leaves to where her brothers were sprinting, neck-and-neck, toward the turn onto their lane. This wasn't the first time that stretch of road had been used as a racetrack. The footbridge was the usual finish line as it would only accommodate one rider at a time.

Susan's somber thoughts vanished. "A race!" she cried. Leaping to her feet, she scrambled down to the far side of the bridge. She planted her feet and stretched her arm high above her head displaying the branch to the contenders. The winner would grab it away from her before leading the way across the bridge.

The team rounded the turn onto the lane, both men riding low and forward, clods of dirt spraying out behind the horses' hooves.

It'll be close, thought Susan squeezing the prize hard.

As they grew larger and larger with their approach, she stared intently and willed her choice of champion toward victory.

Hurry, Samuel! But with that thought, she noticed Samuel pull himself back and up, slowing Elsie, as David continued to push Tillie hard toward the finish. She blinked in disbelief.

What are you doing, Samuel?

Oblivious to Samuel's actions, David flew by snatching the branch from Susan's grasp and thundered across the bridge. He turned with a flourish to confirm his victory to Samuel, who by that time had resumed his racing posture and feigned a frustrated defeat. As David reined in Tillie to gloat, Susan spun around to face him.

"Great job, David!" she hollered. "You're the champion!"

David's face went blank for a second, and then he nodded at Susan and smiled.

She waved to him thinking, *Yes! What a nice big smile. Wait until Rebecca hears.*

As he rode away, she imagined the taste of Mama's apple dumplings, but considered, *you know, that smile was even sweeter. Maybe I'll only eat Rebecca's dessert one day – not three. I've already won the best prize.*

Samuel came alongside her and dismounted to allow Elsie to cool down as he walked her to her stall. Susan ambled alongside. "Why did you let him win, Samuel?" she asked.

"Oh, I think maybe we all won something with that finish, don't you?" he answered. She wrinkled her brow, but understood. "Peace and harmony is often the best prize," he said stroking Elsie's moist smooth neck.

"Yes," Susan sighed and nodded. "I have to agree."

"Saddle up," Samuel said grabbing her waist. "Watch your arm now." He swept her up onto his horse.

"Elsie won't mind taking a sweet passenger like you as far as the barn. Oh, and here's a little something *süssigkeit* from the fair." He grinned pulling a maple sugar candy from his pocket.

Little Cate could not remember a better day. Town fairs were always great fun, but with her baby sister at home, she had Mama nearly to herself. Sitting between her parents on the seat of the wagon, she had pinched her eyes shut to try to hold on to the wonderful feelings forever, but each sway of the wagon made her head feel heavier and heavier until it rested against her mother's lap and her body drooped in sleep. Catherine laid her arm tenderly across Cate's back.

Daniel watched them, pictured the rest of his family in the back and tenderly shook Bessie's reins to urge the mule homeward. David and Samuel had gone on ahead of them two miles earlier. Daniel's breathing eased and his squared shoulders relaxed as he surrendered to a rare sense of contentment.

Polly and Rebecca sat crossed-legged opposite each other in the wagon bed studying the webbed network of strings called a Cat's Cradle laced through Rebecca's ten fingers as she held her hands up in front of her face with the palms facing each other.

"Are you ready?" asked Polly. Rebecca nodded her head.

"Now, watch carefully," Polly continued as she lowered her fingers delicately into the crisscross pattern. "I pinch the string here and here and bring my hands under yours and up through the holes and . . ." She lifted the puzzle intact onto her hands leaving Rebecca's empty.

They grinned. "Now, it's your turn." Rebecca adjusted her position on the rough boards to be as steady as possible and peered at Polly's hands reviewing what she would attempt.

In another corner of the wagon, John was helping Jacob count the clay marbles he had won in the shooting competition as they replayed the skillful moves John had taught him. Deeming himself past the age of playing marbles, John had given his prized collection to the younger Jacob for his last birthday along with the promise to coach him to a respectable standing as a marble shooter among the local boys.

As Jacob carefully funneled the polished marbles into his leather pouch and tied it shut with a rawhide string he said, "Sean was the only one who walked away with more marbles than me."

"And at least six of them were mine," moaned Edward Lehman who was riding his family's horse alongside the wagon.

"I'll be glad to show you a few moves that might help you win them back," offered John. "Stop by the house after you get the leather strapping from Papa for your father. I'll be there taking care of the firewood or at the barn helping Jacob with the milking or bedding down Bessie. It won't take very long. You'll be able to make it home before sundown."

"Thank you, John. I'll do that. I'll be a better match for you next time, Jacob," Edward promised.

As Daniel pulled hard on the right reins and started up the family lane, Catherine said to Polly and Rebecca, "You girls be extra helpful with supper tonight. Elizabeth and Susan have been minding the household most of the day and have earned a rest."

"Yes, Mama," they answered.

"Whoa, Bessie," said Daniel as they reached the tannery. "Edward and I will stop here and take care of business. John, you take the wagon the rest of the way so everyone can get started on evening chores." As the wagon slowed, John climbed onto the bench and took charge of the mules. Daniel stepped down to the lane and Edward Lehman slid off of his horse to follow him.

Daniel had taken only two steps toward the tannery when he turned back to the wagon. "Oh, by the way, Polly, George Schmucker asked to stop by tomorrow evening to speak with me. Said he would be here about an hour before dusk, as soon as he has put in his hours as apprentice to his uncle. I told him it would be my pleasure." Without waiting for a response he continued on his way. He didn't want Polly to catch him smiling.

Polly could hardly believe her ears. It wasn't until Susan hugged her that she allowed herself to accept what she had been waiting and praying to hear for so long. She returned Susan's squeeze and over her sister's shoulder, she caught Catherine's eye where she sat on the wagon seat.

"Oh, Mama, is it true?"

Catherine smiled and nodded. Cate lifted her head from Catherine's lap at the disruption. "Well, hello, Sleepyhead. We're almost home."

Cate rubbed her eyes and lay back down mewing, "But I don't want to stop dreaming yet."

"Two more minutes," Catherine cooed as John flicked the reins and Bessie made her way toward the cabin.

Samuel and David strode from the barn toward home and the beginning of the end of another day. Susan stopped to tidy Elsie and Tillie's tack and to throw some fresh hay into the stalls before starting out the door after them.

She had taken only a few steps when she spied Edward Lehman riding his horse at a leisurely pace from the tannery toward the barn. There was no tactful way to avoid him. *What's Edward doing here?* She wondered, trying not to admit that her face felt suddenly warm.

"Hello, Susan," Edward said touching the brim of his hat and pulling the horse to a stop as he drew near.

"Hello, Edward," she answered with what she dearly hoped was a steady voice, but she couldn't be sure. "What a surprise. What brings you here this late?"

Edward dismounted. He fumbled with the reins and did his best to address her calmly, though he couldn't be sure he looked calm. "I'm on my way home from the fair and I stopped by to get some new leather straps from your papa. The tack for our plow didn't weather very well this winter. I'm bringing over a sack of celery seed tomorrow for trade."

Susan smoothed her apron with her good arm. "Yes, we need to be planting that for Samuel's wedding feast. Sarah Provines' family lives in town and they don't have much land for farming."

"That's right, I remember. The seed I'm bringing over is from the crop we planted for my sister Anna's wedding two years ago." As the conversation progressed, Edward's mind felt steadier. He noticed Susan fussing over her apron and suddenly remembered her accident. "Oh, I nearly forgot, is your arm healing well? You had quite an adventure, I hear."

"Yes. Thank the Lord for George Schmucker and Mukki. It could have been much worse." She held up her splinted limb. "My arm should be right as rain in a few weeks. I can't wait."

"I'm really glad to hear that, Susan."

In the awkward silence that followed, they both began to perspire more than they would have liked. Then the sense of the situation struck Susan. "But, what are you doing here at the barn. The leather goods are down at the tannery."

"Oh, I've been there already." Edward pointed to the bundle tied to his saddle. "I'm supposed to meet John here so he can give me some tips on marble shooting. His coaching helped Jacob do really well at the fair today. Sorry, you couldn't go."

Darn, he thought to himself. *Marbles – wish it were something more grownup. I don't want to sound like a child, not to Susan.*

"Well, he should be here soon. The cows didn't wander very far today," she said.

Now, what? she thought, with that topic exhausted. *I can't just stand here like a child.* She straightened her back and smiled.

Now, what do I say, Edward thought. *I can't just stand here like a child.* Then he finally blurted, "So, I'll just wait here then."

"*Gut.* I'll just get on up to the house to help with supper," she added as she moved past him toward the house. "Good-bye."

"Good-bye," he answered as she moved right beside him.

They turned their heads and were startled by how close together they stood. They both snapped forward and moved ahead struggling not to seem rattled and determined not to look back. As much as they wanted to, they didn't.

Once they were a safe distance from each other they relaxed and smiled to themselves.

-22-

New Beginnings

Susan froze when the wooden step creaked under her bare foot as she descended from the loft in the dark hours of very early morning, long past midnight. She couldn't sleep, but she didn't want to wake anyone, didn't want to try to explain what was keeping her awake. The night painted the house in shades of muted gray with black corners and dark recesses. The rectangular windows glowed with the light of the full moon. The beams cast tilted angles of dim rays across the long table that bounced off the worn rim of the long-handled tin dipper hanging beside the kitchen pump. The lingering aroma of the corn mush supper that had been served later than usual because of the busy day still clung to the rafters. She felt the heavy air hugging her as she deliberately placed each footfall on her way across the room to the smoldering hearth – the slowly pulsing heart of the house.

Mukki, curled up at her usual post by the fireplace, raised her head at Susan's approach, but stirred no further. Susan lowered herself into the halo of warmth cast by the

 glowing embers nestled under the dark cinders and sat beside the spaniel. "Shh," she shushed ever so faintly looking at Mukki and holding her finger to her lips. The dog resumed her original repose with a deep sigh.

"Susan?" her mother whispered from behind.

"Yes, Mama," she replied in hushed tones not turning her head. She knew her mother would have questions – 'Are you all right?' – 'Why are you still awake?' – Questions she either didn't want to or couldn't answer. Still, as much as she regretted losing her solitude, the sound of her mother's voice made her long for her embrace as well.

But mothers are often wiser than their children know. Catherine simply sat down behind Susan, wrapped her arms tenderly around her daughter and waited. Susan leaned gratefully into the warm familiar cocoon her mother offered.

After some minutes Susan said, "What will happen to our log house after we move, Mama?"

"It will be taken down," she explained softy. "It has served us well for many years. It has seen all of my children born and some, bless them, pass on to heaven. It has watched us laugh and cry, kept us warm and safe, stood strong and has asked little in return. But its time has passed and something new must take its place. Change is hard sometimes, but time is the master. As we grow older – grow up – things must change. Remember that very soon Samuel and Polly will be leaving to live in their own homes. But even if we stayed here in our little log home, they would be leaving. Things would still change."

"And I'm happy for them both, really I am, but I'm sad, too," Susan whimpered. "It's hard to think our cabin won't be here anymore."

"As long as we remember it, it's not really gone, *Liebchen*. In fact, Samuel will be using these very shutters on his new cabin, and perhaps the kitchen pump, too. And, I plan to use some stones from this very hearth to border the new front walk."

"Really?"

"Absolutely. And the new house won't look nearly as cold when we fill it with so many things from here – the blankets and dishes and spinning wheel and cook pots. And Mukki will still lie down by the hearth each night to sleep. You'll see."

She grasped Susan's shoulders and turned her around to face her. "Now, off to bed before the rest of the household wakes up." She pulled her to her chest. "Feeling better?"

"Yes, Mama. Thank you." They helped each other up and took a last look at the embers. "How do you know so many things, Mama? Just the right things to say?"

"Oh," Catherine said, "if only that were true. I pray each day for the Lord's guidance and I try to remember all of the wise things that have been told to me in my growing up and through all of the changes in my life since I was just a babe. Something Omah Stoner often said is one of my favorites. 'Cherish the past. Anticipate the future. Embrace the present moment. Give God reverence always.' So far it has served me well. Our family has been very blessed and we need to give thanks each and every day."

"Now," she added looping her arm through Susan's and leading her to the foot of the loft steps, "*Gute nacht.*" Catherine kissed her child's smooth, warm cheeks. "*Suß Träume, Liebchen.*"

"Sweet dreams to you, Mama."

As Susan crept up the stairs, Catherine slipped back to her bed behind the curtained alcove.

Susan wriggled carefully into bed between Rebecca and Cate. Their measured breaths didn't miss a beat. As she drifted into the sleep that had eluded her earlier, her mother's words echoed – *Cherish the past. Anticipate the future. Embrace the present moment. Give God reverence always.*

A Family Tapestry

Glossary

auger	- tool for boring holes in wood
baffles	- a screen to regulate flow in a butter churn
barter	- to trade or exchange
bevy	- a large group
blaspheme	- to speak with a lack of respect for God
cadence	- a rhythmic pattern or pace
calico	- light cotton fabric; a three-colored cat
calloused	- having no sympathy; hard, thick skin
camphor plaster	- large, foul-smelling patch to treat a cold
carcass	- dead body of a meat animal
caustic	- capable of burning or eating away
chamber pot	- bedroom vessel used as a toilet
contagion	- disease that spreads easily
cooperage	- a business that produces wooden barrels
deciduous	- trees that lose leaves in the fall
fallow	- farmland left unplanted
fermented	- to age or change with a chemical reaction
flax	- plant with fibers used to make linen cloth
gristmill	- a mill for grinding grain
haggle	- to bargain
homespun	- rough fabric made of wool or linen
hominy	- shell of corn kernel with inner seed removed
inebriated	- drunk, intoxicated
John Barley Corn	- whiskey made from fermented corn
keelers	- containers for catching sap from maple trees

A Family Tapestry

kiln - a furnace for making lime by burning rocks

Linsey-woolsey - fabric made of linen and wool

Mason - skilled workman who builds with stone

millpond - man-made pond for powering a gristmill

millstone - large, circular stones used to grind grain

pallet - a small, hard bed

parboiled - partially cooked

parchment - paper made from sheep or goatskin

percolate - to ooze or trickle through

perennial - a plants that grows back every year

permeate - to penetrate; to spread throughout

pilfer - to steal in small quantities

porcine - related to swine/pigs

porridge - thick soup of boiled grain and milk

poultice - large medicated patch to treat illness

prodigious - extraordinary, enormous

ramshackle - rickety; ready to collapse

rounders - a children's game similar to baseball

sampler - a piece of needlework with letters or verses

spiles - small spouts used to drain sap from trees

succulent - full of juice; a thick, juicy plant or leaf

symmetry - balanced, equal sides opposite each other

tenaciously - stubbornly; holding on tightly

tinker - a traveling merchant and mender

vanity - being full of pride; conceited

whitewashed - painted white with a water and lime mix

Recipes for Featured Dishes

Fastnachts (Raised Doughnuts)

1 ¼ cups milk	3 eggs, beaten
¼ cup shortening	¾ cup sugar
1 teaspoon salt	¼ teaspoon nutmeg
1 small yeast cake	4 1/12 to 5 cups sifted flour

Scald the milk, add shortening and salt.

Cool milk until it is lukewarm; then add crumbled yeast cake and stir.

Gradually add 2 2/3 cups sifted flour, beating batter thoroughly.

Put in warm place and allow to stand until full of bubbles.

Mix sugar with nutmeg and combine with beaten eggs.

Stir into first mixture and then add remaining flour.

Knead well, cover and let rise in a warm place for about 1 hour.

Turn out lightly on floured board and roll ¾ inch thick.

Cut with doughnut cutter or biscuit cutter shaping into a ball or make into twists.

Cover with a thin cloth and let rise on board until top is springy to touch of finger.

Drop into hot fat with raised side down, so the top side will rise while the under side cooks.

Drain on absorbent paper.

Yields 3 dozen.

Raised doughnuts are delicious if dipped in a syrup made by boiling the following together for 5 minutes: 1 cup sugar, ¾ cup water and 1 tablespoon white syrup.

Hasenpfeffer

8 to 10 pieces of dressed rabbit or pheasant	1 teaspoon salt
	¼ teaspoon pepper
¼ cup fat	½ teaspoon allspice or cloves
1 medium-sized sliced onion	½ cup vinegar
2 heads garlic	1 can tomato puree
2 bay leaves	

Roll pieces of meat in flour and sprinkle with salt and pepper.
Fry until golden brown.
Place in baking pan or casserole and add onion slices, seasoning, vinegar and tomato puree.
Let simmer or bake at 350 for 1 to 1 ½ hours.

Snitz un Knepp (Apples and Dumplings)

1 ½ pounds cured ham or 1 ham hock
2 cups dried apples
2 tablespoons brown sugar

Wash dried apples, cover with water and soak over night.
In the morning, cover ham with cold water and cook slowly for 3 hours.
Add apples and water in which they soaked.
Add brown sugar and cook 1 hour longer.

For knepp or dumplings:

2 cups flour	1 egg, beaten
3 ½ teaspoons baking powder	2 tablespoons butter
½ teaspoon salt	¼ to ½ cup milk

Sift together dry ingredients.
Stir in beaten egg and melted butter.
Add milk to make a batter stiff enough to drop from a spoon.
Drop batter by spoonfuls into boiling ham and apples.
Cover pan tightly and cook dumplings for 10 to 12 minutes.
Do not lift cover until ready to serve.

Serves 8.

About the Authors

Marie Lanser Beck is a former journalist and historian who has written and edited two volumes of veterans' stories and assisted Sen. Edward W. Brooke in writing his memoirs (*Bridging the Divide: My Life*, Rutgers University Press, 2007).

Maxine Beck has a bachelor's degree in education and a master's degree in English. She is a former high school teacher with 17 years of experience teaching advanced English and writing.

Both have been associated with Renfrew Institute for Cultural and Environmental Studies in Waynesboro, Pennsylvania for many years. Marie has served on the board of directors of the Renfrew Museum and Park, as well as the Renfrew Institute. Maxine currently serves as president of the Renfrew Institute's Board of Directors.

About Renfrew Museum and Park

Renfrew Museum and Park in Waynesboro, Pennsylvania preserves the Royer farmstead and interprets Pennsylvania German farm life on a 107-acre site not far from the Mason-Dixon Line, 65 miles from Washington, D.C. and Baltimore, Maryland. The Royer Family's 1812 stone farmhouse and several of the outbuildings described in *The Royers of Renfrew* have been preserved and are open to the public.

Made in the USA
Charleston, SC
18 October 2011